"WILDLY FUNNY. . . . Just the sort of play Oscar Wilde might have written had he lived in 1990s Manhattan and taken aim at an epidemic that was decimating his circle of friends. . . . For all its fun, *Jeffrey* captures the strained social tenor of Manhattan life as it is lived right now perhaps more acutely than any play."
—STEPHEN HOLDEN, *New York Times*

"A frank, fearless comedy about an attractive gay man who swears off sex out of fear and frustration amid the AIDS crisis. . . . A fantastical, picaresque landscape that includes a demonic pop psychology guru and a seedy safe-sex club." —*USA Today*

"In daring to laugh, then to cry, it reveals itself as a cunning twist on the old-fashioned Broadway-style comedy. . . . Rudnick lays out the panorama at double time: a game show, a Gay Pride march, a gay bashing, a taste of rough trade, a vision of Mother Teresa— oh, yes, and a square dance. All with unfettered wit and a lot of heart. Who could ask for anything more?" —*Time*

"THE HOTTEST TICKET OFF-BROADWAY . . . Even with AIDS lurking in the background, *Jeffrey* sparkles. . . . Mr. Rudnick . . . has come up with some of the funniest lines and deftest gimmicks onstage today. . . . {He} is a master of one-liners." —*Wall Street Journal*

"A DAZZLING, BITTERSWEET TRAVELOGUE ABOUT GAY NEW YORK. . . . I don't expect to see a funnier play this year."
—*New York Daily News*

PAUL RUDNICK has received the Obie Award, the Outer Critics Circle Award, and the John Gassner Award for Outstanding New American Play for *Jeffrey*. He is also the author of *I Hate Hamlet*, which was produced on Broadway and is currently being performed in Canada, Brazil, Australia, New Zealand, and throughout the United States. His other plays include *Poor Little Lambs*, which also received the Outer Critics Circle Award, *Raving*, and *Cosmetic Surgery*. He has also written two novels, *Social Disease* and *I'll Take It*, and the script for the movie *Addams Family Values*. His essays and articles have appeared in *Vanity Fair*, *Esquire*, *The New York Times*, *Vogue*, *Spy*, and other publications. He is a graduate of Yale University.

# Paul Rudnick

# Jeffrey

A PLUME BOOK

*PLUME*

*Published by the Penguin Group*
*Penguin Books USA Inc., 375 Hudson Street, New York, New York 10014, U.S.A.*
*Penguin Books Ltd, 27 Wrights Lane, London W8 5TZ, England*
*Penguin Books Australia Ltd, Ringwood, Victoria, Australia*
*Penguin Books Canada Ltd, 10 Alcorn Avenue, Toronto, Ontario, Canada M4V 3B2*
*Penguin Books (N.Z.) Ltd, 182–190 Wairau Road, Auckland 10, New Zealand*

*Penguin Books Ltd, Registered Offices:*
*Harmondsworth, Middlesex, England*

*First published by Plume, an imprint of Dutton Signet,*
*a division of Penguin Books USA Inc.*

*First Printing, February, 1994*
*1 3 5 7 9 10 8 6 4 2*

*Lyrics to "Nice Work If You Can Get It" used by permission of Warner-Chappell Music.*

*CAUTION: Professionals and amateurs are hereby warned that* Jeffrey *by Paul Rudnick is fully protected under the copyright laws of the United States of America, the British Commonwealth, including the Dominion of Canada, and all other countries of the International Copyright Union and Universal Copyright Convention, and are subject to royalty. All rights, including professional, amateur, motion picture, recitation, lecturing, public reading, radio and television broadcasting and the rights of translation into foreign languages are strictly reserved. Particular emphasis is laid on the question of readings, permission for which must be secured from the author's agent in writing. All inquiries concerning rights to* Jeffrey *should be addressed in writing to the author's agent, Helen Merrill, Helen Merrill, Ltd., 435 West 23rd Street, Suite 1A, New York, NY 10011, USA.*

 REGISTERED TRADEMARK—MARCA REGISTRADA

LIBRARY OF CONGRESS CATALOGING IN PUBLICATION DATA
Rudnick, Paul.
Jeffrey / Paul Rudnick.
p.   cm.
Play.
ISBN 0-452-27120-7
1. Gay men—New York (N.Y.)—Drama.   I. Title.
PS3568.U334J44   1994
812'.54—dc20          93-21034
CIP

*Printed in the United States of America*
*Set in Garamond Light and Helvetica Condensed*

*Designed by Steven N. Stathakis*

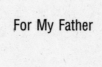

For My Father

# Introduction

*Jeffrey* began as the story of a supporting character in another play I was writing; the character had a different name, but he had given up sex, in response to ten years of the AIDS crisis, the frustrations of safe sex, and the dementia of romance in general. This abandonment of sex suddenly struck me as one of the essential romantic conflicts of our time, and also as a classic plot for a romantic comedy—in short, the character and his quandary demanded their own play. As others have pointed out, the renunciation of love and physical contact has served such playwrights as Aristophanes, in *Lysistrata*, and Shakespeare, in *Love's Labour's Lost*; but while these are both fine works, their authors did not benefit from the satiric fodder of red ribbons, hoedowns for AIDS, and memorials hosted by Siegfried and Roy.

I had no idea how audiences would respond to *Jeffrey*, whether they'd be willing to accept repartee and big-time Gershwin amour amid the nightmare of AIDS. But I knew that any portrait of Manhattan life in the nineties would have to be a blend of the highest farce and the most devastating tragedy, laced with the gay style that has allowed a ravaged community to survive with its wisecracks and wardrobes intact. I wanted to capture the insanity of the AIDS era, and the valor of those who manage to find love and double-ply cashmere between, and even during, hospital visits, marches, and eulogies. I thought of my friend Eric, triumphantly chain-smoking during his final days on earth, because who would dare tell him to quit? I thought of a memorial at which the deceased's answering-machine tape was played, and an ACT-UP meeting at which an earnest young woman demanded that funds be raised to purchase rubber dental dams (a safe sex device) for the indigent citizens of El Salvador; and I thought of an actor I knew who'd run into his agent while the agent was being happily humiliated in a trough at an S&M club. I thought of phone sex and gay bashing and a transsexual acquaintance who had simultaneously become a lesbian, been accepted at law school, and been diagnosed as mildly schizophrenic. And I tried to think beyond these immediate events to some more universal theory of how love and death can be understood only by developing a truly exquisite sense of humor.

*Jeffrey* was written fairly quickly, and then extensively rewritten over the course of 1992. Christopher Ashley, who was to direct the play's initial production, organized a series of readings; *Jeffrey* would not have been possible without his infinite patience, perfect comic pitch, and general genius. Harriet Harris played three roles at the earliest reading; her supreme talent caused me to write her an additional five roles, and to found a religion in her name. During these readings, and during rehearsal at the WPA Theater, I struggled to achieve a balance of comedy and sorrow, to construct a roller coaster; I wanted audiences to find laughter where least expected, and tears that were neither easy nor exploitive.

*Jeffrey*'s production at the WPA will remain one of the most blissful experiences of my personal and professional life. My last play had been *I Hate Hamlet*, and those with tabloid memories will recall the tumultuous nature of its Broadway run, which included the play's star taking out after another actor with a sword. On *Jeffrey*, everything somehow went right: casting director Andrew Zerman led us to select a dream ensemble; the director was my ideal partner in crime; and the theater, under the leadership of Kyle Renick, was supportive, cozy, and ever adaptable to a script that changed hourly. Several theaters had refused to produce *Jeffrey*, fearing that it was just a bit too much, or a lot too much; Kyle agreed to a production within minutes after reading it. I treasure the days I spent in Kyle's CD-lined grotto of an office, as he, Chris, and I would debate the merits of having a character appear dressed in a costume from *Cats*, the possible inclusion of a scene set in the back row of the New York State Theater during Act I of *The Nutcracker*, and the notion of calling in favorite porn stars to audition for supporting roles.

*Jeffrey* had a particularly fiendish final dress rehearsal: there were technical delays, script troubles, a thousand snags which convinced me that the play was a fiasco. The first preview occurred on New Year's Eve, and I experienced what I now regard as the highest form of happiness—relief. The audience went with the play, even when shocked by their own continual laughter. John Michael Higgins was an irresistible Jeffrey; his personal charm and buoyancy kept the crowd's sympathy, even as his character made one wrong decision after another. When Tom Hewitt, the dreamboat playing Steve, announced that he was HIV positive, the theater fell silent; the audience was convinced that the play was no longer a comedy, and yet seconds later they were howling again.

Edward Hibbert and Bryan Batt, as Sterling and Darius, basically enslaved all in attendance; playing a decorator and his chorus-boy lover, they were both giddy and heroic. A critic or two later accused me of writing gay stereotypes, as if decorators and chorus boys should be banished from the stage. But Sterling and Darius are by far the sanest and wisest characters in the play, and in my opinion their flamboyance only enhances their courage. Edward was pure steel in his final hospital scene, which made his grief far more moving; and Bryan's natural optimism and effortless skill were all I had dreamed of for the play. When Bryan said "It's still our party," regarding life in the age of AIDS, the audience both wept and smiled, and the moment never became a lecture or a platitude.

The play's other central scene is that involving Father Dan, the libidinous priest whose counsel Jeffrey seeks. As a nice Jewish boy, I never found this scene shocking; others have felt differently. I never intended this episode as Catholic bashing; Father Dan is a deeply spiritual man trapped in a world and a church that often make little sense, and offer scant real hope or comfort. I reworked this scene endlessly, with the help of Richard Poe, who played Father Dan with a magnetic blend of vaudevillian panache and Old Testament fury. Richard and John Michael Higgins are both of Irish Catholic stock, so their input was authentic, although I was forced to advise Richard that if he played the scene, he would just have to accept the fact that he was going to hell. Richard also gently persuaded me to abandon the conceit of taking Father Dan one step further and having him revealed as a gay Jewish priest. I agree wholeheartedly with Father Dan's exaltation of sex and musical comedy; his lust is meant to bolster his humanity, not to indicate corruption.

Many people have asked me about the inclusion of Mother Teresa in the play's action; they assume her presence to be a touch of pure fantasy. Her appearance is actually one of the more autobiographical references in the play. Several years back, I purchased a carved antique sidechair at a shop on Bleecker Street; the chair was expensive, and wildly unnecessary. As I carried it into the street, Mother Teresa walked by. I later discovered that she was staying in the neighborhood, and having her cataracts removed at nearby St. Vincent's Hospital; she also ran a downtown hospice. At the time, however, I construed her stroll as pure omen, as a warning for me to stop wasting my money and energy on antique chairs; I recall glancing at the heavens and murmuring, "Okay, I get the point." And no, I didn't return the chair;

I eventually decided that Mother Teresa had been browsing.

*Jeffrey* required a seamless production that could travel from Blockbuster Video to the ballroom of the Waldorf, and ultimately to the observation deck of the Empire State Building. The look and flow of the evening resulted from a combination of the director's ingenuity and his work with an inspired team of designers. Jim Youmans's sets created a kaleidoscopic, Hockney-inspired Manhattan; David C. Woolard's costumes were comic masterworks; and Don Holder's lighting and Donna Riley's sound design kept the play's many scenes alive, glowing, and precise (Don's full moon over the Chrysler Building, accomplished on a preschool-allowance budget, never failed to enthrall). Special mention should also be made of Patrick Kerr and Daryl Theirse, who rounded out our cast of nonchalant chameleons, and of Peter Bartlett, who dazzled as an early cast replacement.

The production team had expected walkouts and anger from offended audience members; we were almost looking forward to a little controversy. But none arose: audiences of every age, gender, and sexual preference responded to the play, and people seemed particularly grateful for its hopeful nature. AIDS has been an unimaginable catastrophe, and its savagery continues; the political and medical establishments have been at times viciously ignorant and agonizingly slow to take action. The personal reaction has been far more affirmative; I hope that *Jeffrey* is a tribute to the enduring wit and infinite compassion of the gay community, and to the heterosexual friends and families of that community. Gay men and women have organized to battle an epidemic and to care for its victims; rarely has a group evidenced such style amid so much suffering. AIDS has never been an exclusively gay plague, but the accomplishments of the gay community must not be denied.

My father died of lung cancer in August of 1992; he did not live to see *Jeffrey* produced. When it became apparent that he would not be around to see the play onstage, I gave him an early draft to read. His support of the play, and the support of my mother and brother, have meant the world to me. My father's death was agonizing and instructive; I learned that there are no rules for such events, no correct behavior. My family has always emphasized humor and attempted to avoid self-pity. During his last days, my father was in great pain, and he demanded to die. When the doctors told him that they couldn't just bump him off, he said, in a rather disgruntled tone, "Well, if I can't die, then I want new batteries for my hearing aid." The family burst into laughter; my father looked surprised and then joined in. Death and illness are far from my favorite pastimes; jokes and personality are my preferred antidotes. A wisecrack is not an evasion but a weapon; smart remarks can defeat even a hospital's green-gowned terror. A snappy comeback, or a paisley ascot, or a yellow tulip, preserves humanity; as long as my father could joke, he was still my father, and not just a patient.

I have written other plays and books, but *Jeffrey* is the work that has been most satisfying to me, the piece in which my own personality is most evident—which means, of course, that if you hate the play, lunch would not be a good idea. Up until now my career has been one of self-education; I've been teaching myself to write by making some fairly sizable mistakes as publicly as possible. With *Jeffrey* I felt some sense of progress, or at least a lessening of embarrassment. Luckily I have been blessed with a group of insatiably supportive and wantonly generous friends; for their allegiance over the years, and their willingness to subsidize my Snickers habit, I would like to thank Kim Beaty, Christopher Clarens, Jerry Eaderesto, Adrienne Halpern, Lynn Hirschberg, Jay Holman, Nathan Lane, William Ivey Long, Albert Macklin, Candida Scott Piel, Scott Rudin, Todd Ruff, Peter Schifter, Alison Silver, and Wendy Wasserstein. I would also like to thank my agent and friend, Helen Merrill, who hates to have her name mentioned, and the amazing team of producers who moved *Jeffrey* to the Minetta Lane Theater for a commercial run: Thomas Viertel, Richard Frankel, Steven Baruch, Jack Viertel, Mitchell Maxwell, Alan Schuster and Peter Breger. These men were unstintingly generous, imaginative, and deeply committed to the play; I'm not sure why, but *Jeffrey* has never managed to attract anyone I'm not crazy about.

I hope that anyone reading *Jeffrey* enjoys it, and understands it. It's a play about sex as an invaluable form of human contact, and it's a play about the victory of love, friendship, and sweaters over death. At a critical point in the action, Sterling decries "the limits of style." I hope that style has no limits; for me, style is a human being who says, "I will wear a feather to the funeral. I will dare to be happy."

—PAUL RUDNICK
*May 1993*

# Jeffrey

*Jeffrey* opened on January 20th, 1993, at the WPA Theatre in New York City, Kyle Rennick, Artistic Director, Donna Lieberman, Managing Director, with the following cast:

| | |
|---|---|
| JEFFREY | *John Michael Higgins* |
| MAN #1 IN BED, GYM RAT, SKIP WINKLY, CASTING DIRECTOR, WAITER IN HEADDRESS, ACOLYTE #2 WITH DEBRA, MAN IN JOCKSTRAP, THUG #2, DAVE, ANGELIQUE | *Patrick Kerr* |
| MAN #2 IN BED, GYM RAT, SALESMAN, THE BOSS, ACOLYTE #1 WITH DEBRA, MAN IN CHAPS, THUG #1, FATHER JULIAN, SEAN | *Daryl Theirse* |
| MAN #3 IN BED, GYM RAT, DON, TIM, DAD, FATHER DAN, CHUCK FARLING | *Richard Poe* |
| MAN #4 IN BED, DARIUS | *Bryan Batt* |
| MAN #5 IN BED, STERLING | *Edward Hibbert* |
| MAN #6 IN BED, STEVE | *Tom Hewitt* |
| WOMAN IN BED, SHOWGIRL, ANN MARWOOD BARTLE, DEBRA MOORHOUSE, MOTHER TERESA, SHARON, MOM, MRS. MARCANGELO | *Harriet Harris* |

DIRECTOR   *Christopher Ashley*
SET   *James Youmans*
COSTUMES   *David C. Woolard*
LIGHTING   *Donald Holder*
SOUND   *Donna Riley*
WIGS AND HAIR   *David H. Lawrence*
MUSICAL STAGING   *Jerry Mitchell*
CASTING   *Johnson-Liff & Zerman Casting*
PRODUCTION STAGE MANAGER   *John Frederick Sullivan*

The production of *Jeffrey* subsequently moved to Off-Broadway, where it opened at the Minetta Lane Theatre on March 11, 1993. The only production change was the additon of:

PROJECTION CONSULTANT   *Wendall Harrington*

# Act One

---

*The play takes place in a wide variety of locations, all of which should be suggested as simply as possible. The staging should be fast-paced and fluid, always a few steps ahead of the audience.*

*As the play begins, we see a series of slides projected on the front curtain or scrim, accompanied by a lush, moody Gershwin score. The slides include various ultraromantic views of the Manhattan skyline, the streets of Greenwich Village, and, finally, the windows of an appealing brownstone. It is late at night.*

*JEFFREY is in his thirties, attractive and well put-together. He is an innocent; he is outgoing and optimistic, cheerful despite all odds. JEFFREY believes that life should be wonderful.*

*In half-light, we see two men making love, and then:*

JEFFREY: Ooh! Oh, oh, I'm sorry!

MAN #1: What?

JEFFREY: It broke.

*(The lights come up fully on JEFFREY and MAN #1 in bed, center stage.)*

MAN #1 (*panicking*): It broke?

JEFFREY (*reassuring*): Don't worry.

MAN #1: It broke?

JEFFREY: It's okay.

MAN #1: It broke?

JEFFREY: Do you have another?

MAN #1: On the table—the wicker basket.

JEFFREY (*looking in the wicker basket*): It's empty.

MAN #1: Don't you . . . ?

JEFFREY: That was my last one. What should we do?

(MAN #1 *turns away but remains in bed.* MAN #2 *pops up in bed. The full cast will gradually emerge from the bed, in the manner of clowns piling out of a tiny circus car. Their route of entry will be disguised by the bed's sheets and blankets. As each actor appears, he or she will remain in the bed, which will become quite crowded.*)
(MAN #2 *has a too-sincere, gooey personality.*)

MAN #2: Let's just cuddle.

JEFFREY: Cuddle?

MAN #2: Like little bunnies.

JEFFREY: Bunnies?

MAN #2: Or like little babies.

JEFFREY: Babies?

MAN #2: Can we?

JEFFREY (*agreeably*): Well, okay.

(*They begin to cuddle.*)

MAN #2: Isn't this better?

JEFFREY: Than what?

MAN #2: Than sex.

JEFFREY: Sure.

MAN #2: I wuv you, Mommy.

(JEFFREY *pulls away.* MAN #3, *a hustler, very slick, pops up in bed. He has a smooth, sexy style.*)

MAN #3: Just relax.

JEFFREY: Gee, I've never paid for sex before.

MAN #3: Just tell me what you want. I'll do anything. (*He strokes* JEFFREY*'s face.*) Hey, you're hot. (*Very bored and professional:*) Okay, I am so turned on now. Let's do it all. Let's get wild. Let's burn down the fuckin' house. Just tell me what you want.

JEFFREY (*excited*): I want to have sex!

MAN #3 (*after a beat*): You're nuts.

(MAN #4 *pops up in bed.* JEFFREY *embraces him.*)

MAN #4: Don't you just adore sex?

JEFFREY: I do!

MAN #4: Even nowadays, isn't it just the best thing ever?

JEFFREY: Oh, yeah!

MAN #4: I always have a great time, even with being careful!

JEFFREY: That's incredible!

MAN #4: I just don't like you.

(MAN #5 *pops up in bed. He is rather imperious.*)

MAN #5: Yes?

JEFFREY (*handing him some papers*): Here's my latest medical report.

MAN #5 (*inspecting the papers*): Um-hmm.

JEFFREY (*handing over a form*): And here's the results of my blood test from a month ago.

MAN #5 (*wary*): A month ago?

JEFFREY (*handing him another form*): Last week.

MAN #5: Last week?

JEFFREY (*handing him still another form*): This afternoon.

MAN #5 (*as he checks* JEFFREY*'s throat, eyes, and the glands under his jawline*): Um-hmm. I'll also need the name of your internist, your most recent X-rays, your passport, and a list of all of your previous sexual contacts.

JEFFERY: Well, okay, but isn't that a little extreme?

MAN #5: Do you *want* the apartment?

(MAN #6 *pops up in bed. His body is heavily draped in Saran Wrap, head to toe. He also wears rubber surgical gloves and a surgical mask.*)

JEFFREY: Are you ready?

(MAN #6 *nods yes.*)

Do you feel safe?

(MAN #6 *nods yes.*)

I'm just going to stand way over here—*way* over here—and maybe I'll . . . jerk off.

(MAN #6 *looks suspicious and makes a warning noise through his surgical mask.*)

(*Trying to be cooperative:*) Okay! I won't touch myself! Or you! I'm just going to look at you and—have erotic thoughts. I'm wearing eight condoms, and I won't come! I swear! I promise!

(MAN #6 *nods okay, a bit doubtfully.*)

(*Very carefully, very soothingly:*) Okay . . . here we go . . . this is totally safe. I'm just going to look at you, that's right . . . one, two, three . . .

(JEFFREY *turns and looks at* MAN #6. MAN #6 *panics and screams through his surgical mask.*)

(JEFFREY *refuses to give up and speaks eagerly to the group on the bed:*)

Can we—?

MAN #1: No!

JEFFREY: Oh, but maybe just—

MAN #2: No!

JEFFREY: Oh, oh, but how about just under the—

MAN #3: No!

JEFFREY: And we'll be really, really careful—

MAN #1 AND MAN #6: No!

JEFFREY: And we'll stay totally aware at all times—

MAN #4, #5, AND #6: No!

JEFFREY: But *please*—

ALL THE MEN EXCEPT JEFFREY: No!

JEFFREY: But I swear, I promise—

ALL THE MEN EXCEPT JEFFREY: NO!

JEFFREY: But just for one tiny little second—

ALL THE MEN EXCEPT JEFFREY: NO! NO! NO!

(*A* WOMAN *pops up in bed; she is lovely and soft-spoken, in a silk negligée.*)

WOMAN: Hi.

ALL THE MEN, INCLUDING JEFFREY (*after a beat, a bit shocked*): *NO!*

(EVERYONE EXCEPT JEFFREY *collapses onto the bed, as if asleep or unconscious.*)

JEFFREY: Oh my God, oh no, I wonder if maybe it's really happening! You can feel it coming—oh my God, maybe from now on . . .

(ALL *the people on the bed rise up.*)

ALL: NO MORE SEX!

(JEFFREY *climbs out of bed. Lights down on the bed and everyone in it.* JEFFREY *steps forward and begins to get dressed. He speaks to the audience.*)

JEFFREY: Okay. Confession time. You know those articles, the ones all those right wingers use? The ones that talk about gay men who've had over five thousand sexual partners? Well, compared to me, they're shut-ins. Wallflowers. But I'm not promiscuous. That is such an ugly word. I'm cheap. I *love* sex. I don't know how else to say it. I always have—I always thought that sex was the reason to grow up. I couldn't wait! I didn't! I mean—sex! It's just one of the truly great ideas. I mean, the fact that our bodies have this built-in capacity for joy—it just makes me love God. Yes!

But I want to be politically correct about this. I know it's wrong to say that all gay men are obsessed with sex. Because that's not true. All *human beings* are obsessed with sex. All gay men are obsessed with opera. And it's not the same thing. Because you can have good sex.

Except—what's going on? I mean, you saw. Things are just—not what they should be. Sex is too sacred to be treated this way. Sex wasn't meant to be safe, or negotiated, or fatal. But you know what really did it? This guy. I'm in bed with him, and he starts crying. And he says, "I'm sorry, it's just—this used to be so much fun."

So. Enough. Facts of life. No more sex. Not for me. Done!

And you know what? It's going to be fine. Because I am a naturally cheerful person. And I will find a substitute for sex. Sex Lite. Sex Helper. I Can't Believe It's Not Sex. I will find a great new way to live, and a way to be happy. So— no more. The sexual revolution is over! England won. No sex! No sex. I'm ready! I'm willing! Let's go!

(*Lights up on* GYM RAT #1. *He is working out, wearing a Walkman. We hear the music on his Walkman—hip-hop.*)
(*Lights up on* GYM RAT #2. *He is working out, wearing a Walkman. We hear the music on his Walkman—throbbing disco.*)

(*Lights up on* GYM RAT #3. *He is working out, wearing a Walkman. We hear the music on his Walkman—soaring grand opera.*)
(*The* GYM RATS *will continue their workouts during the following scene.*)
(JEFFREY *bounds into the gym, wearing workout clothes.*)

JEFFREY: It's the answer! I'll pour all my physical needs into working out! Endorphins, not hormones! No sex! Just sweat!

(JEFFREY *is now standing beside a barbell resting on supports over a workout bench.*)

Can I get a spot?

(STEVE, *a good-looking, extremely sexual man in his thirties, turns around.* STEVE *is a master at outrageous, successful flirtation; he knows what he wants.*)

STEVE: You got it.

JEFFREY: Oh my.

STEVE (*referring to the weights*): How much do you want on?

JEFFREY: Oh, forty-fives are fine.

STEVE: I just joined. Do you like it here?

JEFFREY: Oh yeah, a lot. (*He lowers his voice to a more masculine pitch.*) Yeah.

STEVE (*offering his hand*): Steve.

JEFFREY: Jeffrey. (*Lowering his voice:*) Jeff.

STEVE: Are you okay?

JEFFREY: Sure. (*He giggles from nervousness.*) I'm sorry, I'm butching it up. I don't know why I'm doing that. I guess it's to seem sexier—you know, more masculine. (*In an exaggeratedly nelly voice:*) This is the way I really sound. (*In his normal voice:*) I'm sorry.

STEVE: No, don't be. We all do that. Change our personalities, to seem . . . hotter. I'm doing it right now.

JEFFREY: Are you?

STEVE: Technically, we haven't even met yet. (*Putting out his hand:*) Steve.

JEFFREY (*shaking* STEVE*'s hand; romance is now clearly in the air*): Jeffrey.

STEVE: So, do you want to . . . do your set?

JEFFREY: Oh. Yes. Sure.

(JEFFREY *lies down on the weight bench.* STEVE *spots* JEFFREY *on the bench press, monitoring the weight.* STEVE*'s crotch is now directly over* JEFFREY*'s face.*)

STEVE: Ready?

JEFFREY: Oh yeah.

(JEFFREY *starts bench-pressing, as* STEVE *urges him on, rather erotically.*)

STEVE: One . . . two . . . that's right . . . three . . . four . . . you love it . . . five . . . six . . . one more—come on, you're ready—I'm with you—it's so good—don't stop—get it up—pump it—keep it coming, baby, baby, you're there, you're doing it—go, go, go, *owww!!!*

(*The workouts of all the other* GYM RATS *are now in sync with* JEFFREY *and* STEVE; *all of the men have reached a truly orgasmic crescendo. As* JEFFREY's *set ends,* EVERYONE *drops his weights onto the floor with a thud.*)

(STEVE *helps* JEFFREY *lower the barbell back onto the supports.* ALL *of the men in the gym, including* JEFFREY *and* STEVE, *are now panting, exhausted, as if postorgasm.* JEFFREY *remains lying on the bench.*)

STEVE: Cigarette?

JEFFREY: What?

STEVE: Great set.

JEFFREY (*gazing up at Steve's crotch*): You too.

STEVE: What?

JEFFREY (*sitting up*): I mean, thanks. For the spot.

STEVE: Anytime. You look great.

JEFFREY: Thanks. You look . . . terrific.

STEVE: Jeffrey? Jeff?

JEFFREY: Yeah?

STEVE: What would happen . . . if I kissed you? Right now?

JEFFREY: What?

STEVE: Do you want to?

JEFFREY: *Steve* . . .

STEVE: We could drive this place crazy. Everyone's being so butch. We could probably kill people.

JEFFREY: Steve . . .

STEVE: Chickenshit.

JEFFREY: I am not!

STEVE: Then get over here.

JEFFREY: I can't. I have to—

(STEVE *grabs* JEFFREY *and kisses him passionately;* JEFFREY *responds. As the kiss continues, all of the* GYM RATS *look at* STEVE *and* JEFFREY *and, in unison, give a sincere schoolgirl sigh of romantic appreciation.*)

GYM RATS: Awww . . .

(JEFFREY *pulls away.*)

JEFFREY: No! I won't let this happen! No more! I grabbed my stuff and I ran out of there! (*As he runs across the stage and begins to pull on his street clothes:*) I said no sex and I meant it! No backsliding, no loopholes! And I didn't linger in the locker room and tie my shoe five times while he took off his shorts, I didn't admire my knapsack until he got out of the shower, I didn't accidentally have sex with him—oops!—in the steam room! I erased him, from my mind, from every part of my body! Because I am the new Jeffrey, no longer a slave to my libido, to my urges, or to my reputation as the pushover of lower Manhattan. I just left, with a new inner peace, a serenity. I didn't even glance back to see if he was still watching me.

(JEFFREY *glances back;* STEVE *is watching him.*)

No! I won't! I ran right up the stairs and into the street!

(MOTHER TERESA *enters. She wears her distinctive full-length white sari with striped blue trim. We do not see her face, which will remain completely hidden in the veil of her sari.*)

And I see her. Mother Teresa. Near Blockbuster Video. Was it a hallucination? Or was that really her? I read, later on, that she was actually in the neighborhood, having her cataracts removed at St. Vincent's. But was it her? Or just a truly perverse drag queen? A comfortable one? Well, whoever, or whatever, she was, I know an omen when I see one. (MOTHER TERESA *crosses the stage and exits.*) But what does it mean? What's her message? I guess it's—be good. Behave. But—what's good? Okay. First step. Goodbye.

(STEVE *exits.*)
(STERLING FARRELL *enters.* STERLING *is in his thirties or forties; he is superbly regal and beautifully dressed.* STERLING *is never bitchy or cruel; he adores his life and his friends, and exults in stylishness.* STERLING *is an ideal host, generous and amusing. He is* JEFFREY*'s best friend.*)

STERLING: You saw Mother Teresa?

JEFFREY: I swear. She was standing right there. On Eighth Avenue.

STERLING: Well, how did she look?

JEFFREY: I don't know, she was walking. She looked great.

STERLING: Oh, please. She's had work done. I saw her on CNN, she looked sixty.

(*We are now in an elegant men's shop. A* SALESMAN—*pure attitude—is waiting on* STERLING. *He holds up two expensive sweaters;* STERLING *is trying to decide between them.*)

STERLING: Teal? Or slate?

JEFFREY (*as the* SALESMAN *indicates the correct choice*): Teal.

(STERLING *tosses one of the sweaters over his shoulders dramatically, like a cape; the sleeves dangle. He turns his body in profile.*)

STERLING: Can I do this? Or do I look like some sort of gay superhero?

(STERLING *continues to drape the sweater, ever more outlandishly.*)

JEFFREY: Sterling, I think I'm . . . giving up sex.

STERLING: You are? Why?

SALESMAN: Did I miss an issue of *New York* magazine?

JEFFREY: I just think it's time. I love sex so much, but everything's gotten too scary. It's too . . . overwhelming.

STERLING: My dear, what you need is a relationship.

JEFFREY: A relationship?

SALESMAN (*examining* JEFFREY's *shoes; he snorts*): Humph. And shoes.

STERLING: If you had a boyfriend, you could relax. You'd set the rules once and then you'd be fine. That's what Darius and I did, and we've been together for almost two years.

(*The* SALESMAN *helps him into a jacket.*)

Do you like this? I mean, on me?

JEFFREY: But aren't you incredibly frustrated?

STERLING: Of course. I'm hard to fit.

JEFFREY: About sex!

STERLING (*as the* SALESMAN *fusses with him, straightening the jacket, removing lint, etc.*): Darling, love is more than just sex. I mean, even trolls can have sex. What you need is a boyfriend. Someone to nest with, wake up with, just lie around the beach house with. (*Delicately pushing the* SALESMAN *away:*) Sweetheart. Like Darius.

JEFFREY: But Darius is a dancer.

STERLING: Exactly. I said you needed a boyfriend, not a person. I love having a boyfriend. Not having to worry about going out and finding one. Just having someone there, and I mean this in the best possible way, like a wonderful pet that can feed and walk itself. (*Sincerely:*) I mean, I really do love Darius. I love his body, I love his smile, and he has great hands and feet. On some dancers the toes are all smushed, and I mean I would just say "Sorry, Misha, uh-uh, not without socks." And Darius loves me, Lord knows why. (*Handing the jacket to the* SALESMAN:) Charge.

JEFFREY: How is Darius? Is he back in *Cats*?

STERLING: Of course. He's fine. It was just a reaction to the AZT. They adjusted the dosage. He's great.

JEFFREY: Of course.

STERLING: You think I don't know what I sound like. Of course I know. But I have made a decision. I have always been lucky, all my life. Obviously. And I have simply decided to stay lucky. *N'est-ce pas?*

JEFFREY: And you still have sex?

STERLING: Of course. Safe sex. The best.

(*The* SALESMAN *hands* STERLING *a shopping bag with his purchases.*)

Thank you. I mean, Jeffrey—it's just sex.

(*A blast of raucous music is heard. A slide of a handsome, fairly unclothed man might fill the stage.*)

JEFFREY: Just sex? Just sex?

(*Another blast of music, and perhaps more erotic slides.* SKIP WINKLY, *a smarmy, upbeat game-show host, appears, in a flashy tuxedo. He is accompanied by a vapid* SHOWGIRL.)

SKIP: Hi! I'm Skip Winkly, and welcome to "It's Just Sex!"— the show where we explore human sexuality and win big prizes!

(*The* SHOWGIRL *cues canned applause; slides of garish big prizes might appear. The* SALESMAN, STERLING, *and* JEFFREY *now stand behind glittery podiums with buzzers. A sign or slide reads, in Vegas-caliber letters, "It's Just Sex!"*)

SALESMAN: Hi, Skip.

STERLING: Hey, Skip.

JEFFREY: Hi!

SKIP: What a great set of contestants—three gay men! And now let's play "It's Just Sex!" And remember—each question may have more than one correct answer. The most stylish reply wins!

(*The* SHOWGIRL *hands him a card.*)

Here we go—question number one! What seemingly harmless events can now be fatal if they occur during sex?

(*The* SALESMAN, JEFFREY, *and* STERLING *all hit their buzzers, one after the other.*)

SALESMAN: A paper cut.

JEFFREY: Recent dental work.

STERLING: Fluorescent lighting.

SKIP (*pointing to* STERLING, *as the* SHOWGIRL *cues more applause*): Yes, for seventy points!

JEFFREY: I knew that.

SALESMAN: Is my buzzer working?

SKIP: We'll find out! Question number two: Who is your favorite sexual fantasy?

(*The* SALESMAN, JEFFREY, *and* STERLING *all hit their buzzers again, one after the other.*)

SALESMAN: Denzel Washington!

JEFFREY: That guy at the gym.

STERLING: Jacqueline Onassis.

(EVERYONE *stares at* STERLING *questioningly. He rolls his eyes at their obtuseness.*)

To see the apartment.

SKIP (*pointing to* STERLING): Yes again, for seventy points!

JEFFREY (*regarding* STERLING): He was coached before the show.

SALESMAN: I have a slow buzzer!

SKIP: Now, now! It's time for our bonus round, when everything could change, for five *hundred* points! Yes! Here we go: Let's say there's a fella who just loves having sex more than anything. What will happen to him if he suddenly just flat-out dagnabbit *stops*?

(*There is a pause. No one buzzes.*)

SALESMAN (*at a loss*): Gee . . .

STERLING (*at a loss*): Skip . . .

(JEFFREY *is suddenly afire with inspiration, and he hits his buzzer.*)

SKIP: Yes! Gay Man #2, with that hopeful, deluded look!

JEFFREY: Skip, my answer is this: If the fella stops having sex, he will pour himself into his career. And all that rechanneled energy will create incredible career karma, and he'll be a huge success and fantastically happy!

SKIP (*looking offstage*): Judges? What do you say? Will his career compensate? (*He listens to the offstage judges.*) That's absolutely right!

(*The music goes crazy, confetti rains down, and frenzied applause is heard. The* SHOWGIRL *hands* JEFFREY *a dozen roses and places a rhinestone tiara on his head.* JEFFREY *is ecstatic.*)

Wait! Hold it! Just a minute! Judges? (*He listens.*) They have a question—it's nothing really, just a minor technicality. A soaring career can compensate for no sex, but—just what is your career?

JEFFREY: Well, I'm an actor . . . waiter.

(*A pause.*)

SKIP: Which means . . .

STERLING (*stepping out from behind his podium*): I win!

(*The wild music and confetti resume. The* SHOWGIRL *grabs* JEF-FREY*'s roses and tiara and gives them to* STERLING. SKIP, *the* SALESMAN, *and the* SHOWGIRL *all exit.* STERLING *begins to exit, and then notices the audience. He beams, and gives a gracious royal wave as he walks offstage.* JEFFREY *is alone.*)

JEFFREY: Okay, so I'm an unemployed actor. I mean, I'm talented—I think I am. I mean, last week I read for a part, on a TV show!

(*A* CASTING DIRECTOR *appears, very smug and patronizing, seated, holding a clipboard.* JEFFREY *is now at an audition. He tries to be ingratiating.*)

Hi. Jeffrey Calloway.

CASTING DIRECTOR (*handing* JEFFREY *some pages*): Page 33. Police Officer #2. Remember, there are no small parts. Well, actually, there are. All right. You've just burst in on the evil ghetto drug lord. Action.

JEFFREY (*reading from the pages*): "Hold it right there, Diego! Freeze!"

CASTING DIRECTOR (*not happy*): You're a hero. You mean business. Again. Action.

JEFFREY (*a bit more intense*): "Hold it right there, Diego! Freeze!"

CASTING DIRECTOR: You've been hunting him for months. You've finally got him with the goods. But he might have a gun! Action!

JEFFREY (*more intense*): "Hold it right there, Diego! Freeze!"

CASTING DIRECTOR: You hate him! More! Action!

JEFFREY (*pouring it on*): "Hold it right there, Diego! Freeze!"

CASTING DIRECTOR: You loathe him! You scorn him! Make me feel it! More! Prime time!

JEFFREY (*with ultimate fury, his voice squeaking as he uses both hands to aim an imaginary gun*): "Hold it right there, Diego! Freeze! Oh, I just hate you!"

(*There is a pause.*)

CASTING DIRECTOR: Perhaps you'd like to read for our gay role. It's not a caricature, it's a very full human being.

JEFFREY: Sure. The gay role?

CASTING DIRECTOR: Page 68. The neighbor.

(*Lights down on the* CASTING DIRECTOR. JEFFREY *steps forward and addresses the audience.*)

JEFFREY: I got the part. The gay role. Two lines. It was the first time I'd worked in almost a year. Which is why I am a waiter.

(*Another* WAITER *appears, hands* JEFFREY *a starched white service jacket, and exits.* JEFFREY *puts the jacket on.*)

A cater waiter, to be exact. I work for various party outfits—you've heard of them. Glorious Food. Sublime Service. Arugula with Attitude. It's actually kind of fun, because I get to go everywhere, with my shiny black shoes and my garment bag. I've been to private homes, museums, tents in Central Park. It's like gay National Guard.

(*The other* WAITER *reappears. He now wears a bandanna at his throat, cowboy-style. He hands* JEFFREY *a beaded headband with a feather.* JEFFREY *puts the headband on as the* WAITER *exits.*)

JEFFREY: If you're anyone at all, you've ignored me. But I don't mind, because I've tried on your fur.

(*Music begins. Lights up on the ballroom of the Waldorf, decorated with hay, pinto-patterned tablecloths, cacti, and gingham for a country-western theme. Chandeliers descend, also draped in gingham.*)
(STEVE *enters; like Jeffrey and the other waiter, he wears the standard cater-waiter uniform of service jacket, black pants, white shirt, and black bow tie.* STEVE *also wears a red cowboy hat, and perhaps a bandanna.* EVERYONE'*s country-western accessories should appear fairly ridiculous.* JEFFREY *and* STEVE *spot one another.*)

STEVE: Kemo sabe?

JEFFREY: Pardner?

STEVE: Howdy!

JEFFREY: Howdy!

(*As* JEFFREY *and* STEVE *greet each other, the* BOSS *enters. He wears a waiter's uniform and an absurdly oversized cowboy hat. He is a barking bully, perhaps with a Jamaican accent.*)

BOSS: Gentlemen? What do you think you're doing?

JEFFREY (*to* STEVE, *as* JEFFREY *and the* BOSS *exit*): Roundup!

(STEVE *takes his place behind a bar, which is draped with a pinto-patterned tablecloth and set with bottles and glassware. During* ANN MARWOOD BARTLE'*s speeches, he freezes in half-light.*)
(*Lights up on* ANN MARWOOD BARTLE. *She is a giddy socialite in an elaborate ball gown accessorized with a sequined cowboy hat, fringed gauntlet gloves, and a holster with pistols.* ANN *is thrilled beyond measure to be the evening's hostess. She should not be played as southern; think Connecticut lock-jaw.*)

ANN: Good evening, everyone. I'm Ann Marwood Bartle. And I'd like to welcome you to Country-Western Nite here at the Waldorf! A Hoedown for AIDS. Now more than ever we need to combat this terrible disease with funding, education, and gingham. (*She indicates the ribbons on her bodice.*) The red ribbon I wear stands for AIDS awareness. The lavender ribbon is in memory of those who have died. And the diamond spray is a gift of my first husband. And now I'd like to introduce our honorary board of directors at table number one. Hold your applause, please, for Lauren Bacall! Donna Karan! Mr. and Mrs. Henry Kravis! And our very own, the Honorable Mayor David Dinkins. In the chaps.

(ANN *freezes in half-light.* JEFFREY *enters with a tray.*)

JEFFREY: I need a vodka rocks with a twist, and two spritzers.

STEVE (*as he makes the drinks*): I was hoping I'd run into you. I wanted to apologize about the other day, at the gym. I came on a little strong.

JEFFREY: No, you were great. I'm sorry I took off. I was just acting weird. I'm . . . an actor.

STEVE: I thought so. Have I seen you in something?

JEFFREY: Well, did you see "Manhattan Precinct" two weeks ago? Near the end of the show? The gay neighbor? (*Doing sincere, TV-style acting:*) "You know, Karen, I have the same problem . . . with Bob."

STEVE: You were great!

(*The other* WAITER *enters, disgruntled, in a full-tilt Indian headdress and a beaded breastplate.*)

JEFFREY (*Indian-style, to the* WAITER): How.

WAITER (*morose*): Why?

(*The* WAITER *exits.*)

STEVE (*handing* JEFFREY *a drink in a glass shaped like a cowboy boot*): Here you go.

JEFFREY: So—what do you really do?

STEVE: I'm actually, really—a bartender. I sort of acted and I sort of wrote, but mostly . . .

JEFFREY: What?

STEVE: I watch you.

JEFFREY (*pleased*): You do?

(*The* WAITER *reappears.*)

WAITER: He does.

(*The* BOSS *appears.*)

BOSS: Spritzers! Table fifteen!

(JEFFREY *and the other* WAITER *begin to exit to opposite sides of the stage. The waiter pauses and speaks to* JEFFREY, *regarding* STEVE.)

WAITER: Nice work, Little Feather.

JEFFREY: Bitch.

WAITER: Squaw.

(*The* WAITER, JEFFREY, *and the* BOSS *exit. Lights up on* ANN.)

ANN: Is everyone ready to kick up their heels and rustle their petticoats for a new pediatric care unit? Cowhands, cowgals, I give you a very special treat! They've been practicing for—weeks! Let's have a big whoop-ti-aye-ay for Dr. Sidney Greenblatt and his Mount Sinai Ramblers!

(*A raucous country-western square dance tune begins.*)
(JEFFREY *enters with an empty tray. He stares at the dance floor.*)

JEFFREY: Oh my God . . .

(ANN *begins clapping her hands and calling the square dance.*)

ANN: Come on, everyone! Get out on the floor! Here we go! It's a square dance! Yee-haw!

JEFFREY (*to* STEVE): Isn't this bizarre? But I think they're raising a fortune.

STEVE: You're making small talk.

JEFFREY: I need a Bloody Mary and two more spritzers.

STEVE: Am I making you nervous?

JEFFREY: Yes!

STEVE: I like you nervous.

JEFFREY: Why?

STEVE: I have to tell you something. At the gym—that wasn't the first time I saw you.

JEFFREY: It wasn't?

STEVE: No. I've seen you at parties—at the Met, the Armory. You are always chattering away.

JEFFREY: Oh no.

STEVE: What?

JEFFREY: I have this image of myself as . . . a normal person —you know, a guy. But I've always known that I'm secretly really . . . a teenage girl.

STEVE: No! You're great! You're a great teenage girl! The other waiters, they're moody, they're Brando. But you—you have a ball. You belong at the party.

JEFFREY: So do you.

(*The* WAITER *appears in his headdress with a tray.*)

WAITER (à la *Poltergeist*): He's baaack . . .

(*The* BOSS *enters, very angry.*)

BOSS: What is this, a social club? Do you want to be fired?

WAITER: I want my land.

BOSS: Move!

(*The* WAITER *and* JEFFREY *exit, followed by the* BOSS.)

ANN: C'mon, y'all! (*Calling the square dance:*) Swing your partners, round you go, allemande left, then do-si-do! (*Speaking normally:*) Isn't this fun? You little dogies!

(JEFFREY *enters with an empty tray.*)

STEVE: So have we talked enough? Can I see you? After the party?

JEFFREY: I need two glasses of champagne.

STEVE: California?

JEFFREY: No—the good stuff.

(STEVE *starts to pour two glasses of champagne.*)

STEVE: Do you have a lover?

JEFFREY: No.

STEVE: Are you seeing someone?

JEFFREY: No.

STEVE: Do I care?

JEFFREY: You are unbelievable!

STEVE: Find out. (*He laughs.*) I'm sorry, I keep hitting on you. Don't you love this part?

JEFFREY: What part?

STEVE: The part where you can't find out enough, about the other person. Where it's all interesting, where it all seems . . . sexy. First steps.

JEFFREY: To where?

STEVE: To my place. Or your place. Or happiness. Or . . . more.

JEFFREY: You move fast.

STEVE: Catch up. Because if I don't touch you very soon, I may explode.

JEFFREY: You know, until about a minute ago, I had a very strong reason not to go out with you.

STEVE: Which was? No, wait—is it because . . . I'm a cowboy, and you're . . . a waiter?

JEFFREY: We're a proud people.

STEVE: What a shame.

JEFFREY (*toasting* STEVE *with the champagne*): You know, in a better world, I could ask you to square dance.

STEVE: Really? You want to square dance?

(STEVE *holds up his hand. He looks at* ANN MARWOOD BARTLE.)

ANN: Bow to your partner, then once more . . .

(STEVE *snaps his fingers.*)

Cater waiters, take the floor!

(*The lights grow brighter.* STEVE *steps out from behind the bar. He bows to* JEFFREY *and holds out his hand.* JEFFREY *takes* STEVE'*s hand and they begin to dance a rousing, sexy two-step, the cotton-eyed joe.*)
(*As* STEVE *and* JEFFREY *dance, the* WAITER *and the* BOSS *appear and begin to dance as well, as a couple.* ANN MARWOOD BARTLE *joins the number; she might hold a hobbyhorse or fire her pistols. The number becomes a spirited, miniature version of a real Busby Berkeley hoedown complete with square danc-ing and "Yee-haw!"'s. As the number grows in wildness,* STEVE

*begins to remove* JEFFREY*'s clothing; he tosses the discarded items to the other people onstage.* JEFFREY*'s headband comes off, and then his jacket;* EVERYONE *surrounds* JEFFREY *and begins to caress him.*)
(JEFFREY *pulls away from* STEVE *and the group.*)

JEFFREY: No!

(*The music stops abruptly, and* ANN, *the* WAITER, *and the* BOSS *exit.*)

STEVE: You can't do that. This is my fantasy.

JEFFREY (*very torn*): I have to circulate. Table 22.

STEVE: Come on—one more do-si-do.

JEFFREY: I'm working!

STEVE: What is going on with you?

JEFFREY (*very distraught*): We're not allowed to have fantasies! Not anymore!

STEVE: Come on. Let's go.

JEFFREY: I can't!

STEVE: Why not?

JEFFREY: It's . . . I can't explain! It's not you! Yes, it *is* you!

STEVE: What?

JEFFREY: I have to go!

(STEVE *and the hoedown vanish. As they do,* STERLING *enters, wearing something outrageous, perhaps Chinese-inspired lounging pajamas.*)

STERLING: So—he was really cute, this bartender?

(*We are now in* STERLING*'s elegant, if somewhat overdone, Upper East Side apartment.* STERLING *holds a cigarette and a cocktail.*)

JEFFREY: He was fantastic. But I just got so—I don't know! I went nuts!

STERLING: Jeffrey—you are beginning to have a problem.

(DARIUS, STERLING*'s boyfriend, enters, wearing an overcoat.* DARIUS *is a true innocent, a handsome, completely sweet dancer in his twenties.*)

DARIUS: Hi, guys.

STERLING: Hello, sweetheart.

DARIUS: What a day. I am exhausted.

(DARIUS *takes off his coat. He is wearing his costume from* Cats, *which consists of a heavily painted bodysuit, accentuated with yarn and fur, elaborate leg warmers, knitted gauntlets, and a tail. He has already removed his makeup.*)

JEFFREY: Darius—aren't you supposed to leave your costume at the theater?

DARIUS: We were filming a commercial, the new one, and it went late. I got stuck. So you're not having sex anymore.

(DARIUS *sits beside* STERLING; *they are very easy and affectionate with one another. Their love affair is real and lasting. The friendship between* JEFFREY, STERLING, *and* DARIUS *should also be one of great pleasure and devotion.*)

STERLING: What he needs is to fall in love and have a relationship. And then this sex thing will fall into place.

DARIUS: Exactly. Look at us. Look at how happy we are. Don't we make you want to fall in love?

STERLING: You know, sometimes I think we should be on a brochure for Middle America. So that everyone can say, "Oh, look, a wholesome gay couple!"

JEFFREY: Excuse me? You're not wholesome. You're a decorator—excuse me, an interior designer—there, I said it without giggling. And you—you're a dancer. You two are like Martha Stewart and Ann Miller. Which, believe me, I prefer. I hate that gay role models are supposed to be just like straight people. As if straight people were even like that.

STERLING: That's true. I was watching these two guys on "Nightline," on Gay Pride Day? And one of them said, "I'm Bob Wheeler and I'm a surgeon. And my lover is an attorney. And we'd like to show America that all gays aren't limp-wristed, screaming queens. There are gay truck drivers and gay cops and gay lumberjacks." And I just thought, "Ooh—get *her*."

DARIUS: Who's Martha Stewart?

STERLING: She writes picture books about gracious living. Martha says that nothing else matters, if you can do a nice dried floral arrangement. I worship her.

DARIUS: And who's Ann Miller?

STERLING: Leave this house.

(JEFFREY *and* STERLING *freeze.* DARIUS *addresses the audience.*)

DARIUS: Some people think I'm dumb, just because I'm a chorus boy with an eighth-grade education. Well—I live in a penthouse and I don't pay rent. I go to screenings and I take cabs. Dumb, huh? And yes, I'm in *Cats*. Now and forever. And I love it! I do! I figure I'm too young for *A Chorus Line*, and too happy for *Les Miz*. I never got that show—*Les Miz*. It's about this French guy, right, who steals a loaf of bread, and then he suffers for the rest of his life. For *toast*. Get over it!

(*Back to the scene.*)

JEFFREY: That's why I came over. To be convinced about this love-and-relationship bit. Because I do believe that you two are truly in love. You have that special . . . smugness. You're like an advertisement for connubial bliss.

DARIUS: What's "connubial"?

STERLING: It's when one of us can afford a cleaning woman.

(*The doorbell rings.* STEVE *enters, carrying a bouquet of flowers.*)

Steven! Hi!

DARIUS: What a surprise!

JEFFREY: Oh my God . . .

STERLING: Jeffrey, this is Steven. I met him at the showhouse opening, and we talked.

DARIUS: We love him.

STEVE: Hi there.

JEFFREY: How are you?

STERLING: I think they're perfect for each other.

DARIUS: Me too.

STERLING: Steve's a bartender, so they'll have something in common. They can fall in love and cater together—it'll be like "Roots."

JEFFREY (*to* STEVE, *with great, accelerating passion*): Steve— since the first second I saw you, at the gym, I have thought of nothing and no one else. I have fantasized about you— naked—about you kissing me and talking to me and walking down the street with me, and letting you do things to me that I have only permitted with five thousand other men. I think you could change my life and change the world and I would love more than anything to do exactly the same for you and I think it's completely and totally possible that we could be the happiest people alive except—I'm not having sex anymore so—sorry!

(JEFFREY, *in agony, hands the flowers back to* STEVE *and collapses into a chair.*)

STERLING: Wait—you two already know each other.

STEVE: We do.

DARIUS: Oh my God. Oh my God. (*to* STERLING:) It's like I told you. I'm psychic—I can predict boyfriends!

JEFFREY: We're not boyfriends!

(STEVE, STERLING, *and* DARIUS *surround* JEFFREY, *standing or kneeling around his chair.*)

STEVE: Jeffrey, calm down. Stop hyperventilating.

JEFFREY: I can't!

STEVE: Take a deep breath.

(*As conducted by* STERLING, *all four men take a deep breath.*)

Better?

JEFFREY: Sort of.

STEVE: Okay. Now, I want to see you. We can take this as slow as you like. First step. How about—tomorrow night?

JEFFREY: I'm working! Till ten!

STEVE: Afterwards. We'll have dinner.

STERLING (*to* JEFFREY): You must.

DARIUS: You can't ignore the karma. It's too dangerous.

STERLING: You have to get over this bizarre sex thing.

DARIUS: You'll have fun! You'll have appetizers!

STERLING: We're your friends.

DARIUS: We love you.

STERLING: You must obey us.

STEVE: You have no choice, Jeffrey. Dinner?

STERLING (*to* JEFFREY): Dinner?

DARIUS (*to* JEFFREY): Dinner?

JEFFREY: Well . . .

DARIUS: Oh, come on. You're gay. You're single.

STERLING: It isn't pretty.

JEFFREY: Yes!

(STERLING, DARIUS, *and* STEVE *cheer*.)

STERLING (*hugging* JEFFREY): I'm so proud of you! You're dating again!

STEVE: How about the Paris Commune? On Bleecker? I know the maître d'.

JEFFREY: Yes!

STEVE: And Jeffrey?

JEFFREY: Yes?

STEVE: I just . . . okay, just so there are no surprises . . .

JEFFREY: Uh-huh.

STEVE: I'm HIV-positive.

JEFFREY (*after a beat*): Um, okay, right.

STEVE: Does that make a difference?

JEFFREY: No. No. Of course not.

STERLING (*dismissing any doubt*): Please.

DARIUS: HIV-positive men are the hottest.

STEVE: I mean—I'd understand. I'd be hurt and disappointed, but—I just wanted to be clear.

JEFFREY: No, really, it's fine—I mean, come on, it's the nineties, right? The Paris Commune, at ten. I can't wait.

DEBRA MOORHOUSE (*entering from the rear of the theater*): Do you feel lost?

(*Lights down on* STEVE, STERLING, DARIUS, *and the apartment.* JEFFREY *steps forward.*)

JEFFREY: I do!

(DEBRA *is an attractive, vibrant, magnetic woman in a stylish Armani suit. She is in turn ferocious, deeply compassionate, abusive, and a red-hot mama. She is the evangelist as pop star, capable of seducing and threatening her audience—she is the most confident person on earth.)*

DEBRA (*approaching the stage*): So you come to me, and you say "Debra, what can I do to feel better about myself and the world?," and you know what I say?

JEFFREY: What?

DEBRA: Love. It's real. It works. Go for it!

JEFFREY (*to the audience*): Debra Moorhouse—the nation's hottest postmodern evangelist.

(JEFFREY *leaves the stage to watch from the audience.* DEBRA *picks up a microphone and begins to work the crowd—she will use the actual theatergoers as her flock.)*

DEBRA: I'm not here as a priest, or a guru, or as any sort of religious leader. I'm just someone who—likes to talk. And people come to me, and they say, "Debra, I'm in love with an alcoholic, what should I do?" And I tell them, "Don't look to me for answers—look to yourself. And then turn it all over to some higher power, whether that power is simply the collective strength of all the love in the world, or some dude named—Jesus Christ. (*She offers a nod and a salute to heaven.*) Find that source of unconditional love, find that all-encompassing, ultimate love, surrender to that unending, infinite love that will let you say, 'Hey (*her voice shifts from cajoling to a harsh bellow*)—FUCK YOU! Get out of my house until you stop drinking!' " (*She smiles radiantly.*) Let's have some questions. Yes?

(*Various trembling, sincere followers raise their hands, yearning for* DEBRA's *attention.* DEBRA *points to a lucky male* ACOLYTE.)

ACOLYTE #1: Um, Debra, first of all, I just want to thank you for speaking to us tonight . . .

DEBRA: You bet. What's up?

ACOLYTE #1: Well, um, I just broke up with my lover.

DEBRA: Well, we've all been there, haven't we?

ACOLYTE #1 (*puzzled*): With my lover?

DEBRA: Spill, baby.

ACOLYTE #1 (*as* DEBRA *holds out the microphone*): Well, Brad and I have lived together for almost five years, but then he lost his job and started doing cocaine. And he wouldn't look for work and I was paying for everything and we would have these terrible fights and . . . he even tried to hit me with the car. *My* car.

DEBRA: Whoa. Man.

ACOLYTE #1: But I still love him!

DEBRA (*almost laughing, looking at* ACOLYTE #1 *as if he's crazy*): Okay. Okay. Let me cook on this! Okay. Okay. (*Serious again:*) It sounds like you've got a problem with everybody's favorite—low self-esteem. Of course, I don't know you. Maybe you *should* have low self-esteem.

ACOLYTE #1: I just want a relationship.

DEBRA: You want a relationship because you're afraid! It all goes back to mother, doesn't it? Did you love your mother?

ACOLYTE #1: Well, I guess so . . .

DEBRA: Don't lie to me. I'll call her. Did she withhold? Was there . . . abuse?

ACOLYTE #1 (*choked up*): Sometimes . . .

DEBRA: Go see her. Tell her, "Mom, you were chilly."

(ACOLYTE #1 *bursts into sobs;* DEBRA *takes him in her arms.*)

"You forgot my birthday. You beat me with a baseball bat. But I understand. I forgive. I *love* you. And Mom, now you're old. You've got a plastic hip. (*Triumphantly:*) And I've got the bat!"

(*She pushes* ACOLYTE #1 *away.*)

Next?

ACOLYTE #2: Debra, Debra, Debra!!!

(ACOLYTE #2, *another man, is wildly overemotional; he leaps onto the stage.*)

First of all, I want to say that I listen to your audiocassettes at least eight times a day, even in the car on my way to and from work.

DEBRA: Good.

ACOLYTE #2: I've memorized most of them, and sometimes I recite right along with you.

(DEBRA *makes a gesture—"And?"*)

And when I'm home I play the cassettes and I follow along in the book.

DEBRA: I like that!

ACOLYTE #2: I used to be afraid all the time, but you've really helped me to have a life!

DEBRA: *You've* helped you to have a life.

(ACOLYTE #2 *smacks his forehead in recognition of this great truth. He pulls a pair of hand-crocheted baby booties out of his pocket.*)

ACOLYTE #2: And I just wanted to give you this pair of booties that I hand-crocheted for your baby. I know you discourage gifts, except donations, but—I just had to!

(ACOLYTE #2 *hands* DEBRA *the booties. Overcome, he gives her a big wet kiss on the cheek and bounds off the stage.* DEBRA *surreptitiously wipes her cheek with the booties.*)

DEBRA: Well, thank you! These are adorable. But remember, I'm not your idol, your Elvis. Don't worship me—*love* me! Do you see the difference?

ACOLYTE #2: Yeah, okay!

DEBRA: One more!

JEFFREY: Hi, Debra. Debra, I think that sex is the best thing ever, but I've met someone, and he's HIV-positive, and I'm beginning to self-destruct. Now, I'm a waiter, so I can't afford your cassettes, or the mug, or the calendar. Do they mention this problem?

DEBRA: They sure do. It's in my book, chapter ten—cheap waiters! (*She laughs at her joke, then grows serious.*) No, no, no. What you're talking about is evil, am I right? Why is there disease? Why was there a Hitler? (*She holds up the booties.*) Why are these acrylic? Ha! Isn't laughter the best medicine?

(ACOLYTE #2 *gives a halfhearted laugh;* DEBRA *dismisses him.*)

Anyway. Here's the lowdown on evil: it's the absence of love. Ta-da. That's it. Case closed. Where you don't have love, illness makes a home.

JEFFREY: Wait, Debra—are you saying that people get sick because they don't love enough, or because no one loves them?

DEBRA: It may sound simplistic, it may sound cruel, it may sound like I am blaming people for their own illness, and maybe I am. (*Perky again:*) That's Debra!

JEFFREY: Debra, that's crazy.

DEBRA: Think about it! That's it! I'd like to end tonight's session with five minutes of guided meditation. First, I'd like everyone to take the hands of the people on either side of you.

(JEFFREY *holds hands in between* ACOLYTE #1 *and* ACOLYTE #2.)

Close your eyes. Close 'em up. I'd like you to picture yourself as a very young child. You're four or five, you're innocent, open to love. For maybe the last time in your life, you're very appealing. Can you see that child?

ACOLYTE #1: I see him!

ACOLYTE #2: I see him!

DEBRA (*to* JEFFREY): What about you, Mr. I'm-on-a-Budget?

JEFFREY: I . . . I think I see him.

DEBRA: Give him a kiss! Take that child in your arms! Hug him! Squeeze him! Tickle him till he can't breathe and the eyes roll back in his head! Now tell him—"I love you!"

ACOLYTE #1 , ACOLYTE #2, and JEFFREY: I love you!

DEBRA: I can't hear you!

ACOLYTE #1 , ACOLYTE #2, AND JEFFREY (*louder*): I LOVE YOU!

DEBRA: Make him believe it!

ACOLYTE #1 , ACOLYTE #2, AND JEFFREY (*as passionately as possible, howling*): I LOVE YOU!!!

DEBRA (*she can't resist*): Debra!

ACOLYTE #1 , ACOLYTE #2, AND JEFFREY: DEBRA!!!

DEBRA (*suspensefully*): Next week's topic: Dead-end job? Dead-end marriage? Dead-end life? (*Ferociously:*) Stop whining, you big baby! (*With a wave and a smile:*) 'Night!

(*Lights down on* DEBRA *and her acolytes. We hear a phone ring.*)

STEVE'S VOICE (*on his answering machine*): Hi, this is Steve. I'm not in right now. Please leave a message after the beep. Have a great day.

JEFFREY (*to the audience*): I'm sorry.

JEFFREY'S VOICE (*on* STEVE'*s answering machine*): Steve, hi, it's Jeffrey. And . . . I'm working later than I thought. Private party, you know. So can we reschedule? Next week? Maybe? I . . . I can't wait, and I'll call you, and . . . I . . . take care.

JEFFREY (*to the audience*): I know what you're thinking. What a sleazoid, what a major-league, hall-of-fame rat. And maybe you're right. It's just . . . okay, what am I so afraid of? Him getting sick? Me getting sick? Why is the idea of a simple dinner now like an evening of Russian roulette? And I felt like a complete creep, and I couldn't go home and be alone with myself, and I was so horny. Why is that my response to everything?

(*Lights up on a shirtless, well-built* MAN *in a leather biker's jacket and a jockstrap.*)

MAN IN JOCKSTRAP: Hey.

JEFFREY: Why can't I drink?

(*Lights up on another man, in leather chaps and a harness. He speaks in a deep, practiced, ridiculously sexual basso.*)

MAN IN CHAPS: Uh-huh.

JEFFREY: And if I can't touch anyone else, who can I touch?

(*Lights up on* DON, *a tough guy wearing a leather vest over his bare chest, a leather top man's cap, and Levi's.*)

DON: Welcome—to the Lower Manhattan Gentlemen's Masturbation Society. Or, as we call it in our brochure, Beats All. I'm Don, tonight's sergeant-at-arms. Anyone not following our basic guidelines will be asked to leave and, if necessary, ejected. There will be no bodily contact, and no exchange of fluids. Please feel free to remove as much clothing as you like. We are into hot men, mutual getting off, and masculine appreciation.

(*We hear the sounds of a heavy iron door slamming shut and locks turning.*)

The doors have been locked, and we think it's going to be a very hot night.

(*The* MEN *are now standing in separate downlights; the atmosphere is very rough and shadowy. As they speak, in their lowest, huskiest, most seductive voices, the* MEN *pinch, rub, and slap various parts of their bodies.* JEFFREY *stands in the center of the group, a bit downstage. The other* MEN *eye him.*)

MAN IN JOCKSTRAP: Hey.

DON: Hey.

MAN IN CHAPS: Hey.

JEFFREY (*pleasantly*): Hey.

MAN IN JOCKSTRAP: Hot bod, man.

DON: Real hot.

MAN IN CHAPS: Uh-huh.

JEFFREY: Okay . . .

MAN IN JOCKSTRAP: Nice tits, man.

DON: Hot tits.

MAN IN CHAPS: Uh-huh.

JEFFREY (*starting to rub his chest, tentatively*): Hot.

DON: Nice butt, man.

MAN IN JOCKSTRAP: Hot fuckin' *butt.*

MAN IN CHAPS: Uh-huh.

JEFFREY: Thank you.

MAN IN JOCKSTRAP: Hot *bubble* butt.

JEFFREY: Very much.

DON: I want to see you touch that butt.

MAN IN JOCKSTRAP: Touch that hot butt.

MAN IN CHAPS: Uh-huh.

JEFFREY: Okay . . .

(*The* MAN IN CHAPS *has started to slap his own butt with both hands.* JEFFREY *starts to rub his own butt.*)

DON: That's right.

MAN IN JOCKSTRAP: Hot fuckin' butt!

MAN IN CHAPS: Uh-huh.

JEFFREY (*growling*): Yeah . . .

(EVERYONE *but* JEFFREY *begins to rub his own crotch*.)

MAN IN JOCKSTRAP: Do it, man.

DON: Touch that dick.

MAN IN CHAPS: Uh-huh.

JEFFREY: Touch it?

(JEFFREY *begins to rub his own crotch. He continues to rub his butt with his other hand*.)

DON: That's right.

MAN IN JOCKSTRAP: Go for it, man!

MAN IN CHAPS: Uh-huh.

JEFFREY (*as he rubs his crotch and his butt*): Why do I feel like—I'm on the subway? This isn't working, not for me. I wonder if I can just kind of . . . slip out . . .

(JEFFREY *stops rubbing himself. He tries to leave. The* OTHER MEN *do not approve*.)

DON, MAN IN JOCKSTRAP, MAN IN CHAPS (*very threatening*): *UH-UH!*

(*The* OTHER MEN *begin to encircle* JEFFREY, *coming closer and closer*.)

JEFFREY: Oh my God . . .

DON: Take 'em down!

JEFFREY: What?

MAN IN JOCKSTRAP: Let's see that butt!

JEFFREY: Guys . . .

DON: Come on, man!

MAN IN JOCKSTRAP: Here we go! Take 'em down! Rip 'em down!

DON: Gettin' hot!

MAN IN CHAPS: Uh-huh!

(*As the* MEN *begin to unbutton their jeans, we hear a shrill blast on a whistle.* EVERYONE *freezes.*)

STERLING: Stop that!

DARIUS: Leave him alone!

(STERLING *and* DARIUS *have entered, wearing black T-shirts with huge pink paw prints on them. They also wear pink berets and silver whistles on thongs around their necks. They confront the men from the masturbation club, who scamper away. The lights grow bright again.*)

STERLING: We are the Pink Panthers!

(STERLING *and* DARIUS *strike a dramatic pose as conquering heroes.*)

JEFFREY (*very entertained*): You are?

STERLING: We just got off our shift. We're part of a citizens' patrol to prevent gay bashing. We patrolled with five other guys, from Christopher to Bank Street.

DARIUS: From Seventh Avenue to the river. And we have whistles, and walkie-talkies.

(STERLING *displays his walkie-talkie as if it were in a showroom.*)

JEFFREY: I'm so impressed!

STERLING: We're keeping the streets safe. It was Darius's idea.

DARIUS: I wanted to do something.

STERLING: Something with a T-shirt. Don't you love it?

(STERLING *and* DARIUS *twirl and pose, modeling their T-shirts with great flair.*)

I'm sorry, those students in Tiananmen Square were very misguided. Where were the graphics? All it would've taken was one silk-screen. Mao with a *Ghostbusters* circle. (*He demonstrates the circle on his chest.*)

DARIUS: Or that *Miss Saigon* doodle.

STERLING: We heart cultural freedom.

DARIUS (*admiring his T-shirt*): These are going to be very rare. We have to change our name.

JEFFREY: Why?

STERLING: MGM has started a lawsuit. They own the rights to all the *Pink Panther* movies and they claim it's a copyright infringement.

DARIUS: Even though we are a non . . .

STERLING and DARIUS (STERLING *helps* DARIUS *with the phrase*): Profit . . .

DARIUS: . . . organization to prevent violence.

STERLING: They claim it's not homophobia, but you know it is. So we're testing all the other studios. We've come up with a great new name for our patrol.

JEFFREY: What?

STERLING: Fantasia.

DARIUS: So how was your date? Where's Steve?

JEFFREY: He . . . I had to cancel. I just got off work.

DARIUS: Did you call him?

JEFFREY: Of course. I left a message on his machine.

DARIUS: Left a message? Call him again! He's a doll!

(*The beeper on* STERLING*'s walkie-talkie goes off.*)

STERLING (*into his walkie-talkie, in a very butch voice*): Hello. Pink Panthers. (*More social:*) Oh, hello, darling.

DARIUS: Is someone in trouble?

STERLING (*listening to the walkie-talkie, very upset*): Really . . . No . . . Oh no.

JEFFREY: What?

STERLING: We have to get over to Washington Square right away. It's Todd, that huge bodybuilder from the gym!

DARIUS: Oh, no. Not Todd!

STERLING: In shorts!

(STERLING *and* DARIUS *blow their whistles and exit at a gallop.* JEFFREY *watches them go.*)
(STEVE *enters from the opposite side of the stage.*)

STEVE: Jeffrey.

JEFFREY: Steve! Did you—?

STEVE: I got your message. That party. You poor guy. But I was all revved up, so I went out anyway. Dancing.

JEFFREY: Great. I . . . I . . .

STEVE: I know.

JEFFREY: No, I really . . .

STEVE: Jeffrey, it's not the first time this has happened to me. You freaked. Cold feet.

JEFFREY: That's not true . . .

STEVE: Stop it. I can understand, about the HIV thing. It's not easy. But I don't like lying about it. I don't like . . . politeness. Not anymore.

JEFFREY: I'm sorry. I just—couldn't deal with it. Not right now.

STEVE: Okay. Fine. (*A beat.*) There's lots of things we could do. Safe things. Hot things.

JEFFREY: I know . . .

STEVE: But you just . . . don't want to.

JEFFREY: I'm sorry.

STEVE: You're sorry. I'm sorry. It's the new national anthem. You said that you . . . thought about me. That you . . . fantasized.

JEFFREY: I know.

STEVE: Do you? Still?

JEFFREY (*after a beat*): Yes.

STEVE: But . . . Jesus Christ. Jesus *Christ.* I can take being sick, I can fucking take dying, but I can't take this.

JEFFREY: You should have told me.

STEVE: I did.

JEFFREY: Sooner! Before . . . things happened!

STEVE: Before I kissed you!

JEFFREY: Yes!

STEVE: Okay! You didn't have all the . . . information. Okay. I've been positive for almost five years. I was sick once, my T-cells are decent, and every once in a while, like fifty times a day—an hour—I get very tired of being a person with AIDS. A red ribbon. So sometimes . . . I forget. Sometimes I choose to forget. Sometimes I choose to be a gay with a dick. Can you understand? At all?

JEFFREY: Yes.

STEVE: Can I . . . forget again?

JEFFREY: No.

STEVE: Can I do something, say something, that will let this happen? I want you, Jeffrey. I may very well even love you. And that means nothing? That should beat anything. That should win!

JEFFREY: I know.

STEVE: Then why are you the one with the problem? Why do I get to be both sick and begging? (*A beat.*) Why won't you kiss me?

(JEFFREY *moves toward* STEVE. *They are about to kiss.* JEFFREY *pulls away.*)

JEFFREY: I'm sorry—no, I'm sorry I said I'm sorry! I'm sorry you're sick! And I'm sorry I lied! I'm sorry it's not ten years ago, and I'm sorry that life is suddenly . . . radioactive!

STEVE (*after a beat, staring at* JEFFREY): Apology accepted.

(STEVE *exits.*)

JEFFREY (*exploding*): I hate sex! I hate love! I hate the world for giving me everything, and then taking it all back!

(*Two* THUGS *appear from the shadows on either side of* JEFFREY.)

THUG #1: What's up?

JEFFREY (*unsure*): Hey.

THUG #2: Are you . . . gay?

JEFFREY (*after a beat*): Mom?

THUG #1: You a faggot?

JEFFREY: Yes.

THUG #2: You queer?

JEFFREY: Please—don't do this.

THUG #1: Suck my dick.

JEFFREY: Do you really want me to do that?

THUG #1: Yeah. No!

THUG #2: Fuck you, man.

JEFFREY: Look, why are you doing this? On Christopher Street?

THUG #1: What is this, like, sacred ground?

JEFFREY: Maybe.

THUG #1: You think you're so special? What are you, one of them fancy faggots? You go to the gym, you got nice friends, you think you're so hot?

JEFFREY: No.

THUG #2: You think you're better than us?

JEFFREY: I'm a waiter.

THUG #1: A waiter? Like at a restaurant?

JEFFREY: Sort of.

THUG #1: They let you touch food? Put your faggoty fingers on it?

JEFFREY: Yes they do. I touch it all the time. I spit in it.

THUG #2: Jesus. What restaurant?

JEFFREY (*sizing up the* THUGS): Pizza Hut.

THUGS #1 and #2 (*very grossed out*): Uck! Damn! Shit!

THUG #1: Let's dust his ass.

JEFFREY: Fine. Kill me. You're the ones who'll suffer. The rest of your lives. Buffet style.

THUG #2: Shut the fuck up.

JEFFREY: You have weapons. So do I.

THUG #1: I got a knife. What do you got?

JEFFREY: Irony. Adjectives. Eyebrows.

THUG #2: Fuck you. Hold him!

(THUG #1 *holds* JEFFREY *while* THUG #2 *punches him in the stomach.* JEFFREY *doubles over in pain. The* THUGS *throw* JEFFREY *onto the ground and kick him. One* THUG *holds* JEFFREY*'s arms while the* OTHER *goes through* JEFFREY*'s pockets.)*

Shit.

THUG #1 (*digging in* JEFFREY*'s pocket*): He's got cash!

(*They hear a distant siren. As the* THUGS *panic,* JEFFREY *bites the leg of* THUG #2.)

THUG #2: Shit, he's bitin' my leg! I'm gonna get AIDS!

(*The siren grows louder.*)

THUG #1: Come on!

(THUG #2 *gives* JEFFREY *one more, particularly vicious kick. The two* THUGS *run off.*)

(JEFFREY *moans. He struggles to sit up.*)

JEFFREY: Shit. Owww.

(MOTHER TERESA *enters. She kneels beside* JEFFREY, *cradling him.*)

Terry.

(MOTHER TERESA *strokes him.*)

Oww. (*To* MOTHER TERESA:) You know, when that asshole started kicking me, I had this horrible stupid thought, this flash, that at least it was . . . physical contact. Well, I think I've found my substitute for sex. A substitute for everything. Bruises. Phone machines. Fear.

(MOTHER TERESA *takes* JEFFREY*'s hand.* JEFFREY *looks up at the night sky. He looks at* MOTHER TERESA. *He begins to sing, a bit of the Gershwins' "Nice Work If You Can Get It":*)

> Holding hands at midnight
> 'Neath a starry sky
> Nice work if you can get it
> And you can get it if you try
> Loving one who loves you
> And then taking that vow
> Nice work if you can get it
> And if you get it
> Won't you tell me . . . how . . .

(*The lights fade.*)

# Act Two

*A slide or sign appears, reading "Sexual Compulsives Anonymous."*
*There is a microphone on a stand at center stage. A MAN enters and moves to the microphone.*

TIM: Hi. My name is Tim, and I am a sexual compulsive.

CHORUS OF OFFSTAGE VOICES: HI, TIM!

TIM: Today I have already performed oral sex on three different people. I can't help myself. I'm an agent.

(TIM *leaves the stage.* SHARON *enters, a clearly depressed woman. She stands at the microphone.*)

SHARON (*with great difficulty*): Hi. My name is Sharon, and I . . . I'm a sexual compulsive.

CHORUS OF OFFSTAGE VOICES: HI, SHARON!

SHARON: Oh, that felt good. (*She takes a deep breath.*) I feel like . . . I'm on my way. Admitting I have a problem is the first step to healing. (*Unconsciously, she begins to stroke the microphone stand, up and down, with her hand.*) Now, for the first time in my life, I feel like I don't need a man to define myself. (*She notices a guy in the front row.*) Hi there.

(SHARON, *very frustrated, leaves the stage.* DAVE *enters and stands at the microphone.*)

DAVE: Hi. My name is Dave, and I'm sexually compulsive.

CHORUS OF OFFSTAGE VOICES: HI, DAVE!

DAVE: I just love sex. Maybe it's because I have a constant erection, twenty-four hours a day. Or because my penis is fourteen inches long.

CHORUS OF OFFSTAGE VOICES (*very interested*): Oooh. Hi, Dave.

(SHARON *reappears, staring at* DAVE, *completely smitten. He nods his head, and she follows him offstage. As they exit,* JEFFREY *enters and stands at the microphone.*)

JEFFREY: Hi. My name is Jeffrey, and I'm . . . just like you.

CHORUS OF OFFSTAGE VOICES: Jeffrey . . .

JEFFREY: I'm a sexual compulsive. But I haven't had sex in almost six months!

(*Applause from offstage.*)

I never even think about sex, not anymore. And I used to . . . be compulsive.

(*More applause and cheers.*)

All because of Billy Kearny. I blame him! That's where it started. He kept daring me. "I dare you to take off your clothes—even your underpants." "I dare you to kiss me—on the mouth." Oh God. Two naked fourteen-year-old boys, in front of the big mirror in my parents' bedroom. I'm having sex. And I'm watching myself have sex. Please don't do that. Please don't stop. (JEFFREY's *memory has become very alive and emotional.*) Stop.

(*Lights up on the full stage.* JEFFREY *is wearing his waiter's uniform. He takes his place behind a long rectangular table covered with a floral chintz tablecloth. There is a silver chafing dish on the table, along with china and linen napkins.*)

JEFFREY (*to the audience*): I'm working. A memorial. Another one. At a townhouse. It's for a curator, at the Met. The speakers are great. His straight brother. His doctor. His gorgeous Italian boyfriend. (JEFFREY *smiles at the boyfriend, across the room.*) Oh, my God, I am so disgusting. Do you know what I'm doing? I'm cruising a memorial.

(STERLING *enters, in a stylish black suit, with a cocktail.*)

STERLING: Oh, please—everybody is. That boyfriend. Carlo. I'm telling you, while Jessye Norman was singing that hymn, everyone was watching *that* him. It's not that we're not sad, it's just . . . there are all these guys here.

JEFFREY: And we've been through so many of them—memorials. Each one more moving and creative than the last.

STERLING: The Gay Men's Chorus doing Charles Ives.

JEFFREY: Vanessa Redgrave reading Auden.

STERLING: Siegfried and Roy.

JEFFREY (*looking across the room*): Who is that? Talking to Darius?

STERLING: It's Todd Malcolm.

JEFFREY: What?

STERLING: You know, from the gym.

JEFFREY: Oh my God.

STERLING: Jeffrey . . .

JEFFREY: He must weigh eighty pounds.

STERLING: He just got out of the hospital.

JEFFREY: He's blind, isn't he?

STERLING: It's a side effect—they think that ninety percent of the vision will return.

JEFFREY: Oh my God.

STERLING: Don't stare.

JEFFREY: Don't stare? When I first came to this city, he was . . . a god. I'd never seen anything like that. I used to watch him, dancing with his lover. People would gasp. (*He begins taking off his service jacket.*) I'm sorry.

STERLING: What are you doing?

JEFFREY: I can't work here. I can't go to one more of these. I can't see one more twenty-eight-year-old man with a cane.

STERLING: Don't be ridiculous.

JEFFREY: What are we doing? Cruising? Giggling? Pretending it's all some sort of hoot? I can't keep passing hors d'oeuvres in a graveyard! I went out with Todd! I just saw him in the hospital, and I don't even recognize him!

STERLING: Stop it!

(DARIUS *enters, in a dark suit, with a cocktail.*)

DARIUS: Hi, guys. Did you see Todd?

STERLING: Of course.

DARIUS: He looks better.

JEFFREY: Darius, Todd is dying!

(DARIUS *faces him;* JEFFREY *realizes his mistake.*)

He's . . . doing okay, I guess.

DARIUS: At least he's out of St. Vincent's. I mean, three months! Remember that collage he made on the wall? With all those Armani ads, and anything with Ann-Margret? (*He realizes something is wrong.*) What's going on here?

STERLING: Jeffrey is just having some sort of anxiety moment.

DARIUS: About Todd, right? It's okay. Do you know what we were talking about? This memorial. The cannoli are frozen. The drinks are watered. And I hated that singer. At my memorial, I want Liza.

STERLING: You are not having a memorial.

DARIUS: I mean, like, in a million years.

STERLING: You are not going to get sick. I thought I'd made that clear.

DARIUS: But I *was* sick. I had pneumonia, and it went away. But I want—the Winter Garden. I do! And I want all the other cats to come out . . . and sing "Darius" to the tune of "Memory." (*He sings, to the tune of "Memory," while making pawlike gestures:*) "Darius, we all thought you were fabulous . . ."

STERLING: Fine. And the service will run for years.

JEFFREY: Sterling!

STERLING: What?

JEFFREY: I mean . . . aren't we all being just a bit much? About all this?

DARIUS: What do you mean?

JEFFREY: I mean—it's a memorial.

DARIUS: So?

JEFFREY: We're making remarks. We're dishing it.

STERLING: Really, darling. Picture mine. And Jeffrey, do re-member—open coffin. They can say it to my face.

JEFFREY (*viciously*): Good idea.

DARIUS: Well, I like it. I mean, cute guys, and Liza, and dish —it's not a cure for AIDS, Jeffrey. But it's the opposite of AIDS. Right?

STERLING: Shh, bow your heads. We're supposed to be pray-ing. (*They all bow their heads.*)

JEFFREY (*to* STERLING): What are you praying for?

STERLING: What do you think? No more disease, no more prejudice.

DARIUS: And?

STERLING (*glancing around*): No more chintz.

NURSE'S VOICE (*on PA system*): Scott Elliman to the front desk —Scott Elliman. Visiting hours are over in fifteen minutes. Fifteen minutes. Regular visiting hours are ten A.M. to four-thirty. And six to eight P.M.


(*Lights fade on the memorial. Lights up on a row of fiberglass waiting-room chairs. There is an exit sign, a sign reading "St. Vincent's," and a metal cart holding an array of medical paraphernalia.*)
(JEFFREY *sits in one of the chairs.* STEVE *enters; he and* JEFFREY *see each other.*)


JEFFREY: Are you following me?

STEVE: Of course, I always follow men into clinics.

JEFFREY: How are you?

STEVE: Still positive. Darn.

JEFFREY: Okay . . .

STEVE: And you? What brings you to St. Vincent's high-profile outpatient facility? White sale?

JEFFREY: Blood test.

(STEVE *grins and crosses his fingers on both hands.*)

STEVE: I'm sorry. There was one thing I never told you. I'm HIV-positive—and obnoxious.

JEFFREY: I knew.

STEVE: Still no acting work?

JEFFREY: No.

STEVE: Still no day job?

JEFFREY: No.

STEVE: Still no sex?

JEFFREY: Steve.

STEVE: You know, Jeffrey, St. Vincent's is not just another Blue Cross pavilion and biopsy barn. Oh no.

JEFFREY: What is it with you?

STEVE: Oh, I don't know. Being here, in my living room, and seeing you—it's a killer combo. It's just got me all a-tingle. What shall I wear?

(STEVE *goes to the medical cart and begins holding up various items. His tone is that of a haughty, scintillating host at a fashion show.*)

What will today's sassy and sophisticated HIV-positive male be wearing this spring, to tempt the elusive, possibly negative waitperson? Let's begin with the basics—a gown! (*With a flourish, he unfurls a green hospital gown and puts it on over his clothes.*) It's crisp, it's cotton, it's been sterilized over five thousand times—it always works. (*He begins to model the gown, as if on a runway.*) It's a go-nowhere, do-nothing look, with a peekaboo rear and (*indicating a bloodstain*) a perky plasma accent. Add pearls and pentamidine, and you're ready for remission!

JEFFREY: Only in green?

STEVE: Please! Green is the navy blue of health care. But it's the accessories that really make the man. Earrings . . . (*He holds two syringes up to his ears and aims them at* JEFFREY.) Careful! Hat . . . (*He places a bedpan on his head as a chapeau; he removes the bedpan and reads the label.*) "Sanicare"! And of course . . . (*He holds up two surgical gloves.*) Gloves!

JEFFREY (*very entertained, applauding*): I'll take it!

STEVE: Cash or charge? (*He pretends to take a charge card from* JEFFREY.) Oh no—but according to this, madam is HIV-negative. This is not for you. This is only for a select few, the truly chic, the fashion plates who may not live to see the fall collections.

JEFFREY: Steve . . .

STEVE: Can I show you something in—a healthy person? Someone without complications? Someone you could bear to touch?

JEFFREY: Look . . .

STEVE: Okay. Okay. Show's over. (*He curtsies.*) Merci.

JEFFREY: Are you all right?

STEVE (*tugging off the gown*): What do you care? Stop being so compassionate. No one's watching.

JEFFREY: Jesus Christ!

STEVE: I'm sorry, I'm a little manic today. And I didn't expect to see you here. I'm being a jerk.

JEFFREY: No, you're fine. I admire your spirit. And your humor.

STEVE: Don't admire me! Fuck me! Admiration gets me an empty dance card, except for the chest X-rays and the occasional march on Washington. Admiration gets me a lovely memorial and a square on the quilt!

NURSE'S VOICE (*on PA system*): Jeffrey Calloway to examining room one—Jeffrey Calloway.

STEVE: Your table is ready.

JEFFREY: Do you want to go first?

STEVE: What?

JEFFREY: I don't mind.

STEVE: Jeffrey, I am not here to see the doctor. Surprise!

JEFFREY: You're not?

STEVE: No, I'm on my way to the tenth floor, to see the AIDS babies.

JEFFREY: Why?

STEVE: As a volunteer. The last time I was up there, there were eight. They were all abandoned, or their parents had died.

And no one would touch them—the nurses were all scared, or busy. The first baby I saw was just lying there, staring, not even crying. But when I held her, she finally smiled and gurgled and acted like a baby. We're all AIDS babies, Jeffrey. And I don't want to die without being held.

(STEVE *exits. Lights fade on the clinic.* JEFFREY's DAD *enters; he is a straightforward midwestern man, in a cardigan and Sansabelt slacks. He is on the phone.*)

DAD: Well, howdy, stranger. (*To offstage:*) It's Jeff!

MOM (*from offstage*): Oh!

JEFFREY: Can you tell if you're having a nervous breakdown? Or do you just wake up in a straitjacket, and notice the bars on the windows? I called my parents.

(JEFFREY *picks up a phone receiver and continues to address the audience.*)

DAD: Well, isn't this a special occasion!

JEFFREY: I love them. I mean, I wasn't kicked out or abused or anything. But they still live in Wisconsin, and we just sort of agree not to get too personal.

DAD: Your mother's right here.

(JEFFREY's MOM *enters, in a cardigan, a wrap skirt, and sneakers. She is wholesome and sensible.*)

JEFFREY: But what if I could really talk to them? What if they really had some answers? Or would that just be too weird?

DAD: So how are things in the Big Apple?

JEFFREY (*into the phone*): Dad—I've stopped having sex.

DAD (*to* MOM): Eileen, Jeff's stopped having sex.

MOM (*concerned*): Let me get on the other line. (*She picks up an extension.*) No sex? You mean just safe sex, don't you, dear?

JEFFREY: No, Mom, I hate safe sex.

DAD: Wrestling with those condoms.

MOM: Water-based lubricants.

DAD: Dry kissing.

MOM: Sweetheart—are you a top or a bottom?

JEFFREY: Mother!

DAD: Have you tried any of those workshops?

MOM: What about a jerk-off club?

DAD: How about—phone sex?

JEFFREY: What?

MOM: Fred, let's help him out. (*To* JEFFREY:) Darling, what are you wearing?

JEFFREY: Jeans and a shirt.

DAD (*very matter-of-fact*): Oh, that's hot.

MOM: That's very hot.

DAD: Are you alone?

JEFFREY: Dad! I am not going to have phone sex with you and Mom!

MOM: Oh, don't be such a stick-in-the-mud. This is your mother. I've bathed you. I've changed your diapers.

DAD: Is that what you like?

JEFFREY (*panicking*): Operator?

MOM: Darling, you can't just resign from the human race. Have you looked at any videos?

JEFFREY: Videos?

DAD: Hard-core. Have you explored masturbation?

MOM: As if we have to ask. Sometimes I never did get into that bathroom.

DAD: We like that new Jeff Stryker film. *Powertool II*.

MOM: Jeff isn't in that one, dear. It's got Lex Baldwin. He's a little short, but he's got beautiful skin. And oh, that scene in the prison laundry!

DAD: I like Jeff. I say stick with the best. *Powertool. The Young and the Hung*. I'm from Wisconsin.

MOM: Dear, do you like it when they shave their assholes?

JEFFREY: Shave their *what*?

DAD: And what about this fellow Steve? Seems very nice.

JEFFREY: Dad—Steve is HIV-positive.

MOM: And a dreamboat. Check the basket.

(JEFFREY *hangs up*.)

JEFFREY: Oh my God. I'm sorry, I'm sorry. That is not really the way it went.

(MOM *and* DAD *switch their phone receivers to opposite ears*.)

DAD: So, you keeping busy?

JEFFREY: Oh yes, I worked five nights last week.

MOM: That big city. It sounds very exciting.

JEFFREY: Sometimes. So how are you? Doing okay?

DAD: A touch of arthritis. Can't complain.

MOM: Have you tried Motrin? We love it!

JEFFREY: No, not yet.

DAD: So—when will we see you again?

JEFFREY: Soon. As soon as I can take some time off. Christmas for sure.

MOM: I love you.

DAD: Take care.

JEFFREY: Dad . . .

(*Lights down on* MOM *and* DAD. *A stained-glass window begins to glow. An altar railing appears. Sacred music is heard. We are in St. Patrick's Cathedral.*)
(JEFFREY *puts on a jacket and kneels at the railing, his back to the audience. He crosses himself, bows his head, and begins to pray.*)
(*A priest,* FATHER DAN, *enters, wearing the traditional collar and full-length cassock. He kneels beside* JEFFREY, *crosses himself, bows his head, and begins to pray. After a moment,* FATHER DAN*'s hand reaches out and grabs* JEFFREY*'s behind.* JEFFREY *stares at the priest, who withdraws his hand. Both men bow their heads and resume praying. Once again* FATHER DAN*'s hand reaches out and grabs* JEFFREY*'s behind, with a great deal of conviction.* JEFFREY *squirms and stares at* FATHER DAN.)

JEFFREY: Excuse me?

(FATHER DAN *rises with great dignity. He stands, and motions with his head.*)

FATHER DAN: Come on.

(FATHER DAN *exits.* JEFFREY, *quite perplexed, follows him.*)
(*Lights down on the altar. Lights up on a storeroom somewhere in the cathedral, with piles of hymnals and a Gothic bench.* FATHER DAN *enters, followed by* JEFFREY. FATHER DAN *is very working-class, a tough, two-fisted guy. He is passionate in his beliefs; he is a dedicated, thoughtful, lusty man, clinging to sanity while surrounded by absurdity and horror. This scene must be played with great ferocity and need; it is not just a chat or debate.*)

FATHER DAN: In here.

JEFFREY: Where are we?

FATHER DAN: A storeroom. Some old hymnals. They need to be rebound.

(FATHER DAN *grabs* JEFFREY *and kisses him.* JEFFREY *pulls away.*)

JEFFREY: Hey!

FATHER DAN: What? What's wrong?

JEFFREY (*stunned*): Excuse me?

FATHER DAN: Is it the collar? Is that a turn-off? Aren't you Catholic?

(FATHER DAN *makes another lunge at* JEFFREY, *chasing him around the room.* JEFFREY *fends him off.*)

JEFFREY: Wait! Are you really a priest?

FATHER DAN: Of course.

JEFFREY: But what's going on? Why did you bring me here?

FATHER DAN: I'm attracted to you. The door's locked.

JEFFREY: Wait—you're a priest? And you cruise guys at St. Patrick's?

FATHER DAN: Yeah! And what were you doing in the pews?

JEFFREY: I was not! Aren't you supposed to be straight? And celibate?

FATHER DAN: Wait—maybe you didn't hear me. I'm a Catholic priest. Historically, that's somewhere in between chorus boy and florist. C'mere.

(FATHER DAN *chases* JEFFREY *again.* JEFFREY *pushes him away with great fury.*)

JEFFREY: No! Get away from me! Don't touch me!

FATHER DAN (holding up his hands, backing off): All right! All right! I won't! What's wrong?

(JEFFREY *tries to pull himself together. During the following speech, his despair, rage, and yearning will overwhelm him.*)

JEFFREY: Two nights ago I was at the ballet, with my friends. It's *Nutcracker.* And it's intermission, and we're walking down this wide marble staircase, and suddenly—Darius falls. He just crumples up, and pitches forward, and keeps tumbling, and his legs are all bent, and there's blood everywhere, and Jesus—he's a dancer! He's just a kid! And he's so dehydrated from some fucking AIDS drug that he can't even stand up! And all the parents are screaming about their kids, and the blood, and we get him into an ambulance, and he's home now, but I've been walking for forty-eight hours! And I finally come here, to church, where I haven't been since I was twelve, and all I keep thinking is—what if it was Steve? How could I love someone, and watch that happen?

FATHER DAN: Wait—who's Darius? Who's Steve?

JEFFREY (*exploding*): Why did He do this? Why did God make the world this way, and why do I have to live in it? You're a priest—you have to tell me! Don't you?

FATHER DAN: All right. If I tell you—if I show you the true face of God—will you listen?

JEFFREY: Of course! That's why I'm here!

FATHER DAN: Will you really listen?

JEFFREY: Yes!

(FATHER DAN *sits* JEFFREY *down*.)

FATHER DAN: First, here's how you see God. He's a Columbia recording artist.

JEFFREY: What?

FATHER DAN: You got your idea of God from where most gay kids get it—the album cover of *My Fair Lady*. Original cast. It's got this Hirschfeld caricature of George Bernard Shaw up in the clouds, manipulating Rex Harrison and Julie Andrews on strings, like marionettes. It was your parents' album, you were little, you thought it was a picture of God. As, I believe, did Shaw. Right?

JEFFREY (*surprised*): Yeah.

FATHER DAN: Well, you were almost there. Because God is on that record. Lerner and Loewe! "Why Can't the English." "Wouldn't It Be Loverly." I'm telling you, the only times I really feel the presence of God are when I'm having sex, and during a great Broadway musical!

JEFFREY: You're nuts.

FATHER DAN: Excuse me? All you people, you're worshipping resurrections, virgin births, Ben-Hur, and I'm nuts?

JEFFREY: I'm talking about a plague! About, I don't know—evil!

FATHER DAN: Yes! Satan! Well, that's another story. I've seen him. He's among us. He's real.

JEFFREY: What? Disease? Hospitals? Fear?

FATHER DAN: *Phantom. Starlight Express. Miss Saigon!* Know ye the signs of the devil: overmiking, smoke machines, trouble with Equity.

JEFFREY (*rising to leave*): Gotta go . . .

FATHER DAN: Why? Because I haven't told you the secret of life, in five words or less? You're getting antsy?

JEFFREY: I need to know!

FATHER DAN: Okay, okay. I am so horny! Do you know what it's like in that confessional? "Father, I abused myself eight times last week." "Father, I'm attracted to my brother-in-law." "Father, I'm having impure thoughts about my soccer coach." Where are the Polaroids? What am I, a mind reader? Say six Hail Marys and bring me his shorts!

(JEFFREY *starts to leave again.*)

Okay, okay—secret of life. All of those people out there, in the pews, they're not so bad, most of them. They're just like you—you just want a few mindless answers, some auto-comfort, and you're a little too uptight for Madame Zora in her storefront. But you've only got one problem—you're completely wrong!

JEFFREY: I am?

FATHER DAN: Of course! Who's your God? Some prissy classroom monitor, nodding at the brown-nosers, and smacking anyone who gets out of line? A God who does what—sends us Mussolini and brain cancer to test us, for our own good? That's not God—that's Aunt Betty with an enema!

JEFFREY: So what—there's no God? It's all just random, luck of the draw, *bad* luck of the draw!

FATHER DAN: Darling, my darling—have you ever been to a picnic? And someone blows up a balloon, and everyone starts tossing it around? And the balloon drifts and it catches the light, and it's always just about to touch the ground, but someone always gets there just in time, to tap it back up. That balloon—that's God. The very best in all of us. The kindness. The heavy petting. The eleven o'clock numbers.

JEFFREY: But what about the bad stuff? When the balloon does hit the ground, when it bursts?

FATHER DAN: Who cares? Evil bores me. It's one-note. It doesn't sing. Of course life sucks; it always will—so why not make the most of it? How dare you not lunge for any shred of happiness?

JEFFREY: With Steve, who's sick? Who I'm afraid to touch?

FATHER DAN: So maybe you need a rubber or a surgical mask or a roll of Saran Wrap! But how dare you give up sex, when there are children in Europe who can't get a date! There is only one real blasphemy—the refusal of joy! Of a corsage and a kiss!

JEFFREY: So what're you telling me? Perk up? Look on the sunny side? Get out more?

FATHER DAN: What's your alternative? When did despair become enjoyable? Grief, yes; tears, of course; but terminal gloom? Who does that help? Even Brecht wrote musicals.

JEFFREY: If you believe all this, all this smile-button gospel, if those people out there have it all wrong—then why did you become a priest?

FATHER DAN: I'm working from within. That's why I have to stick around, kiss a few rings, get to be a cardinal. 'Cause the next time we choose a Pope, I've got the guy.

JEFFREY: What? Who?

FATHER DAN: Tommy Tune! Perfect, huh? Someone upbeat? I know it's nuts, of course it's ridiculous—who could afford him? But that's my church—high kicks to heaven.

JEFFREY (*backing away*): You're no priest! I don't know what you are! You're just some sort of lunatic, dressed up in a priest suit!

FATHER DAN: Isn't that redundant? (*Pursuing* JEFFREY *again:*) Here we go!

JEFFREY: Get away from me!

FATHER DAN: I told you the meaning of life! Now put out!

(FATHER JULIAN, *an earnest young priest, knocks on the door.*)

FATHER JULIAN: Father Maginnis, please! I don't know what to do! You have to help me!

FATHER DAN: All I wanted was a quickie. (*He opens the door.*) Yes, my son?

FATHER JULIAN: Father, Mass is about to begin. The congregation is starting to worry.

FATHER DAN: Oh, all right! Those people! What would happen if I didn't show up? Animal sacrifice?

FATHER JULIAN (*shocked*): Father!

FATHER DAN (*to* FATHER JULIAN): You're new. You'll learn. (*To* JEFFREY:) Think about what I said. Will you do that? And call me?

JEFFREY: I can't.

FATHER JULIAN: Father, the altar boys are in place!

FATHER DAN (*to* FATHER JULIAN): Don't tease.

(FATHER DAN *and* FATHER JULIAN *exit, followed by* JEFFREY. *The scenery for the storeroom begins to vanish. Joyous, irresistible disco music is heard.* STEVE *appears, wearing an official Gay Pride T-shirt. He carries a bullhorn and a clipboard. We hear parade noise.*)

STEVE (*into bullhorn*): The parade is about to begin! The first unit will be as follows: Dykes on Bikes!

(*The roar of motorcycles is heard.*)

Concerned Pan-Asian Bisexuals!

(*A cheer is heard.*)

Black Gay Republicans!

(*There is no response.*)

Hello?

(*A middle-aged woman runs on. She wears a New Jersey Mafia princess look: stretch pants, high heels, bouffant hair, outsize sunglasses, lots of gold jewelry, a quilted lamé bag, and a glitzy sequined sweatshirt with shoulder pads. Animal prints might also be a favorite. She speaks with a nasal Jersey accent; she is rowdy and forthright, clearly a social leader and a take-charge person. She is* MRS. MARCANGELO.)

MRS. MARCANGELO (*to* STEVE): Excuse me! Are you with the parade? I'm lost!

STEVE: No problem. Which group are you with?

(ANGELIQUE MARCANGELO *enters. Angelique is the woman's son, in drag, and they are dressed somewhat alike, overdone and cheery.*)

ANGELIQUE: Ma! Did you find out? (*To* STEVE:) We're marching together.

MRS. MARCANGELO (*sincerely*): I am so proud of my preoperative transsexual lesbian son!

(JEFFREY *enters, carrying a full laundry bag.*)

JEFFREY: Steve.

STEVE: Jeffrey! We're about to start! Who are you marching with?

MRS. MARCANGELO (*to* JEFFREY): Excuse me—could you take our picture? With this nice man?

(*She hands* JEFFREY *her camera and poses with* STEVE *and* ANGELIQUE.)

It's for my album. It's our first parade!

ANGELIQUE: We're going to be on a truck!

STEVE (*to* JEFFREY): Parents of Transsexuals.

ANGELIQUE: Preoperative Transsexual Lesbians.

JEFFREY: Okay . . .

MRS. MARCANGELO: Believe me—

JEFFREY (*snapping the photo*): Smile!

MRS. MARCANGELO: —at first I was as confused as anyone. (*She takes back the camera.*) More confused. When Anthony first came to me—

ANGELIQUE: Angelique, Ma.

MRS. MARCANGELO: You were still Tony, at the time. He said, "Ma, I want to be a woman—I've always felt like one." I said, "What, are you gay?" He said, "No, I'm not gay—I'm a lesbian!"

ANGELIQUE: Exactly!

MRS. MARCANGELO: And my first thought is, when I was pregnant with you, what did I do? Did I Tilt-a-Whirl? Did I bungee jump?

ANGELIQUE: But you didn't judge.

MRS. MARCANGELO: Listen, alone, late at night, I judged plenty. I judged you, I judged me, I said, I don't understand, why does he need this? And you know what made me feel better?

STEVE: What?

MRS. MARCANGELO: Those Summer Olympics. I was watching them on TV, feeling sorry for myself. And they kept showing the parents, of all those girls in the pool, those . . .

ANGELIQUE: Synchronized swimmers.

MRS. MARCANGELO: Exactly. And the parents were all crying, and waving little flags, and I just thought, Hey—if they can be proud of their kids, just because they can stand on their heads in the deep end, then I can be proud of mine!

(STERLING *enters, wearing sunglasses and carrying a large, rolled-up banner.*)

STERLING: Jeffrey! Steven!

(STERLING *and* STEVE *kiss.*)

MRS. MARCANGELO: Look at that—two men kissing! (*She snaps a photo and says to* ANGELIQUE:) Why can't you be like that?

ANGELIQUE: *Ma* . . . do we need sunscreen?

MRS. MARCANGELO (*rummaging through her shoulder bag*): Right here.

STERLING: Has anyone seen Darius? I lost him somewhere near the S&M people. I swear, I saw this terrifying man, wearing a dog collar, a harness, and jackboots, snarling at me. And I look closer, and it's my upholsterer.

(DARIUS *runs in, wearing a T-shirt, shorts, and boots, very excited.*)

DARIUS: Should I get my nipples pierced?

STERLING: What?

DARIUS: I just saw this big guy, totally naked, except for a jockstrap and two big gold rings, right here and here. (*He gestures on his chest.*)

STERLING: For guest towels.

MRS. MARCANGELO: Which group are you with?

STERLING: Gay Men Who Need a Cigarette.

(STERLING *and* DARIUS *unfurl their banner, which stretches between them on a pole. The banner is beautifully lettered and decorated with expensive fringe and tassels.* STERLING *and* DARIUS read aloud the words on the banner.)

DARIUS: "Interior Designers Fight AIDS."

STERLING: "Care with Flair."

(*Loud parade noise is heard—bands, motorcycles, disco, etc.*)

STEVE: We're starting! (*Into bullhorn:*) Parents of Pre-Ops! Prepare to move!

ANGELIQUE (*to her mother*): How do I look?

MRS. MARCANGELO (*tenderly*): Gorgeous!

ANGELIQUE and MRS. MARCANGELO (*protecting their coiffures as they attempt to hug*): Hair!

(*The* MARCANGELOS *exit, very excited.*)

STERLING: Come along, Jeffrey—help with this thing.

JEFFREY (*holding up his laundry bag*): Delicate hand washables—I'll catch up.

DARIUS: All right! (*To* STERLING:) Move it!

(STERLING *and* DARIUS *exit, carrying their banner.*)

STEVE: Dump that stuff. I'll put you on the best float—with the porn stars.

JEFFREY: No, it's okay. I'm not marching.

STEVE: You're not marching?

JEFFREY: Not this year. I can't. I am not an asset to this parade.

STEVE: Jeffrey, I hope this doesn't have anything to do with me. I know I gave you a pretty tough time.

JEFFREY: You didn't.

STEVE: I tried. But it really is good to see you. You look great. And I'm not hitting on you.

JEFFREY: Why not?

STEVE: Oh, Jeffrey.

(*They stare at each other, in an awkward moment of renewed longing.*)

JEFFREY: I should go. I'm meeting someone.

STEVE (*with a leer*): Pardon me?

JEFFREY: My sublet. I hope.

STEVE: Your sublet? Are you moving? Where?

JEFFREY: It doesn't matter.

STEVE: *Where?*

JEFFREY: I shouldn't have said anything!

STEVE: Come on!

JEFFREY: Back to Wisconsin.

STEVE: Wisconsin?

JEFFREY: Not for a month! I have to go . . .

STEVE: Wait a minute!

JEFFREY: It's a very good idea! There are no car alarms, no potholes . . .

STEVE: No parades. What about Sterling? And Darius?

JEFFREY: Don't tell them!

STEVE: *What?*

JEFFREY: I'm going to—I just have to find a spare moment, we've all been so busy . . .

STEVE: You are leaving town? Now?

JEFFREY: Darius is doing much better! He looks great! He's off the intraconozal, he's gained his weight back . . .

STEVE: You are really a piece of work.

JEFFREY (*after a beat*): Yes I am! I'm a shit, and I'm a coward, and I'm a traitor. And I'm running away, just as fast as my frequent flier miles can carry me! Because if I stay here, I will lose it! And how does that help anyone?

STEVE: And what are you going to do? In Wisconsin?

JEFFREY: Live! Breathe! Hide! Until it's all over!

STEVE: Until what's all over? AIDS? Or your life?

JEFFREY (*very distraught*): Either.

STEVE: Good to have known you. A growth experience.

JEFFREY: Okay, look, maybe I'll come back. Who knows? Someday.

STEVE: There is the difference between you and me. In that one word. "Someday." A real luxury item.

(SEAN, *another marcher, enters. He is attractive and appealing.*)

SEAN: There you are!

(SEAN *and* STEVE *kiss.* STEVE *gets rather passionate.*)

STEVE: Sean, this is Jeffrey.

SEAN (*very friendly*): Really? At last! I've heard way too much about you!

JEFFREY: Oh, those tabloids. Are you guys . . . ?

STEVE (*to* SEAN): For what? Two months now?

SEAN (*to* JEFFREY): We met on the parade committee. (*To* STEVE:) They need you. (*To* JEFFREY:) Great to meet you.

(CHUCK FARLING, *a TV reporter, enters, in a blazer and a star-tlingly blond blown-dry hair style. He carries a microphone and speaks to the camera. He is vain and fatuous, very full of himself and his own importance.*)

CHUCK (*adjusting the hidden headset in his ear*): Yeah, I know we've got to cover this thing, but why me? (*Smiling for the camera:*) Good afternoon, this is Chuck Farling, here at Manhattan's some would say notorious Gay Pride March. Homosexuals have made great strides in recent years, and— I'm surrounded by them. Your names?

STEVE: Steve Howard.

SEAN: Sean Bailey.

CHUCK: And are you . . . homosexuals?

STEVE: Yes, Chuck, we are.

SEAN: We are righteous members of the Queer Nation!

STEVE: And you?

CHUCK: No! Oh no, I'm . . . with Channel 9 Action News.

(STERLING *and* DARIUS *enter and spot* CHUCK.)

DARIUS (*crazed*): *Chuck!*

CHUCK: Yes, young man? (*To the camera:*) Another gay marcher.

DARIUS: I love your show! You are so cute! (*Trying to compose himself, for the camera:*) Hi. We're here, we're queer . . . (*unable to control himself*) . . . and we're on TV!

STERLING: Chuck, I'm truly sorry. He gets overexcited.

(STERLING *has been staring at* CHUCK*'s hairpiece.* STERLING *reaches over and touches* CHUCK*'s hair, lightly.* CHUCK *pulls back.* STERLING *reassures him:*)

No, it's working, really.

CHUCK: Spirits are running very high here in Washington Square! (*He spots* JEFFREY.) And here's a regular fellow—why, he could be anyone, your son, your brother, the guy next door. Your name?

(CHUCK *strides over to interview* JEFFREY. DARIUS, STERLING, STEVE, *and* SEAN *all move right along with* CHUCK; *they are all eager to stay on camera. They group themselves behind* STERLING *and* DARIUS*'s banner.*)

JEFFREY: Jeffrey.

CHUCK: And how are you celebrating Gay Pride Day?

JEFFREY: I'm . . . doing my laundry.

STEVE: His laundry! Just like a regular person! You see, all gays are not flamboyant and overtly . . . extreme.

(DARIUS *flamboyantly kicks one leg out from behind the banner.*)

So you're doing your laundry, here on Gay Pride Day.

JEFFREY: Yes, Chuck, I am.

CHUCK (*to the camera*): Provocative.

(*The* MARCANGELOS *enter. They see* CHUCK *and scream.* JEFFREY *exits.*)

MRS. MARCANGELO: Chuck!

ANGELIQUE: Chuck Farling!

MRS. MARCANGELO: We love you!

(*The* MARCANGELOS *run over to* CHUCK *and look into the camera.*)

Hi, Theresa—hi, Mrs. Russamano—it's us! We're on TV! With Chuck Farling!

CHUCK: Well, it seems we have a mother-and-daughter team here with us—is that right?

ANGELIQUE: That's right!

MRS. MARCANGELO: Don't ask.

CHUCK: And what are you ladies doing to celebrate this Gay Pride occasion? Something very special?

ANGELIQUE: You bet, Chuck! We're going to ride on a flatbed truck, for all the world to see!

MRS. MARCANGELO: Because we are proud of who and what we are!

CHUCK: And after the parade?

STERLING (*taking* CHUCK*'s microphone*): Angelique is going to remove her penis.

(*Everyone cheers, as* CHUCK *looks distinctly uncomfortable and motions with a finger across his throat to his film crew—* *"Cut!"*)

NURSE'S VOICE (*on PA system*): Dr. Matthews to ICU—Dr. Matthews. Joel Garber to the front desk—Joel Garber.

(*Lights dim on the parade. Lights up on St. Vincent's waiting room.* STERLING *enters and sits in one of the fiberglass chairs. He is alone. After a beat,* JEFFREY *enters.*)

JEFFREY: How is he?

STERLING: No change.

JEFFREY: Can I see him?

STERLING: No. He won't know who you are. Or talk. It's a coma.

JEFFREY: Do you need anything?

STERLING: No, I'm okay. Where were you?

JEFFREY: Working. My last job. The Hilton. A whimper. Is his mom in there?

STERLING: No. She's back at our place, getting some rest. He doesn't recognize anyone.

JEFFREY: You never know, for sure—

STERLING (*cutting him off*): No he doesn't. He's dead.

JEFFREY: What?

STERLING: Half an hour ago. I . . . that's the first time I've said it. Out loud. A brain hemorrhage. That's why it was so fast. Brain things. That's why three weeks ago, he was marching on Fifth Avenue. With me.

JEFFREY: Sterling, I am so sorry.

STERLING: You're what?

(JEFFREY *tries to embrace* STERLING. STERLING *pulls away.*)

You're sorry? Thank you, Jeffrey. Thank you. Darius is dead. I'm sorry too. (*He takes a breath, and then, sincerely:*) I'm sorry.

JEFFREY: Is there anything I can do?

STERLING (*very straightforward, not emotional*): I wasn't . . . enough. I wasn't important enough. I couldn't snub it. I couldn't scare it off, with a look. I couldn't shield him, with raw silk, and tassels, and tiebacks. The limits of style.

JEFFREY: You loved Darius. He loved you.

STERLING: Jesus, Jeffrey, how can you?

JEFFREY: What?

STERLING: Jeffrey, I don't know why, I'm obviously out of my mind, but right now—no, I don't. I don't hate you.

JEFFREY: You hate me?

STERLING (*standing, moving away*): Jeffrey, perhaps you should just not be here. Just right now.

JEFFREY: Sterling, please—let me help you. What can I do?

STERLING: What can you do? Nothing! You're leaving. You're going away, to . . . someplace insane.

JEFFREY: I can stay. For a few more days.

STERLING: No. Please go. You are not part of this. This has nothing to do with you. You know, Darius said he thought you were the saddest person he ever knew.

JEFFREY (*stunned*): Why did he say that?

STERLING: Because he was sick. He had a fatal disease. And he was one million times happier than you.

JEFFREY (*after a beat*): You loved Darius. And look what happens. Do you want me to go through this? With Steve?

STERLING: Yes.

(MOTHER TERESA *appears. She gestures at* STERLING; *he freezes. She gestures again, and* DARIUS *enters, in a dazzling, all-white version of his* Cats *costume.*)

DARIUS: Jeffrey—guess what?

JEFFREY: Sterling!

DARIUS (*sitting on one of the fiberglass chairs*): You know that tunnel of light you're supposed to see, right before you die? It really happens! The first person I saw was my Aunt Berniece. She had emphysema. She hugged me and she said (*as Aunt Berniece, crossing his legs, taking a drag on a cigarette and speaking in a gravelly voice*), "Darling, can you get me a pair for the matinee?"

JEFFREY (*staggered*): What are you? Some sort of grief-induced hallucination? Are you a symptom? Why did you come back?

DARIUS: To see you. I figured you got here too late, after I was already in the coma. Did you bring me anything?

JEFFREY: Um . . . flowers!

DARIUS (*looking around*): Where?

JEFFREY: I was in a hurry!

DARIUS: Jeffrey, I'm dead. You're not.

JEFFREY: I know that.

DARIUS: You do? Prove it.

JEFFREY: What do you mean?

DARIUS: Go dancing. Go to a show. Make trouble. Make out. Hate AIDS, Jeffrey. Not life.

JEFFREY: How?

DARIUS: Just think of AIDS as . . . the guest that won't leave. The one we all hate. But you have to remember.

JEFFREY: What?

DARIUS: Hey—it's still our party.

(*We hear an orchestra tuning up.* DARIUS *stands.*)

That's the orchestra. I have to go.

JEFFREY: But . . . but is that it? Is that all you can tell me?

DARIUS: Be nice to Sterling.

(MOTHER TERESA *gestures. Gorgeous romantic music begins, perhaps the Gershwins' "Embraceable You."* STERLING *unfreezes. He and* DARIUS *gaze at each other and smile. The music swells.*)

DARIUS: See you! I'm on.

(DARIUS *exits.* STERLING *exits in the opposite direction. The lights change. The skyline of Manhattan appears, beneath a glorious full moon. A railing and perhaps a telescopic viewer appear. The clinic vanishes; we are now on the observation deck of the Empire State Building.)*

*(There is a sports jacket hanging over the railing. A red balloon is also attached to the railing.* MOTHER TERESA *helps* JEFFREY *into the jacket; she checks his appearance. She hands him the balloon. She exits.)*

*(*STEVE *enters, looking around.)*

STEVE: Jeffrey?

JEFFREY: Steve! You showed up!

STEVE: What is this? A scavenger hunt? Am I on a list? "Meet Steve on the top of the Empire State Building"?

JEFFREY: I wasn't sure you'd come, when I left the message. I didn't know if . . . John would let you.

STEVE: Sean. Have you seen Sterling?

JEFFREY: Yeah. He's doing okay. He liked the memorial.

STEVE: So did I.

STEVE AND JEFFREY (*after a beat, they sing softly to the tune of "Memory"*): "DARIUS, WE ALL THOUGHT YOU WERE FABULOUS . . ."

STEVE: Nice balloon.

JEFFREY: It was a gift.

STEVE: And what are you still doing here? I thought you were headed west, or north.

JEFFREY: I need a favor.

STEVE: This is very Hitchcock.

JEFFREY: I have to ask you something.

STEVE: And your phone was shut off. Gay castration.

JEFFREY: Be serious. Can I ask you my favor?

STEVE: I'm here.

JEFFREY: Dump Sean.

STEVE: What?

JEFFREY: Leave him. Tell him it's over. Be really mean.

STEVE: It's a little late for that!

JEFFREY: Why?

STEVE: He's gone. He . . . dumped me.

JEFFREY: He did? *Really?*

STEVE: Oh, calm down. He couldn't take it. The sex. He was exhausted. He's twenty-two.

JEFFREY: Were you upset?

STEVE: Of course!

JEFFREY: A whole bunch?

STEVE: Jeffrey!

JEFFREY: Steve, if I asked you to, could we have sex? Safe sex? Some kind of sex? Tonight?

STEVE: On the top of the Empire State Building?

JEFFREY: Wherever. I needed . . . a moon. You haven't answered my question.

STEVE: Wait a minute! What is this? You think it's so easy? You leave a message, snap your fingers? Jeffrey, I'm still HIV-positive.

JEFFREY: So?

STEVE: So—it doesn't go away! It only gets worse!

JEFFREY: I know.

STEVE: Don't do this. Don't pretend. I will not be your goc deed!

JEFFREY: Oh, you're not. I'm too selfish. I don't want a r ribbon. I want you.

STEVE: Say we have sex. Say we like it. And say tomorrc morning you decide to take off, for Wisconsin!

JEFFREY: I won't!

STEVE: How do I know that?

JEFFREY: Because I'm a gay man. And I live in New York. A I'm not an innocent bystander. Not anymore.

(STEVE *is now somewhat convinced. He studies* JEFFREY *fo: moment.*)

STEVE: So . . . how bad do you want it?

JEFFREY: Find out.

STEVE: I like this. This is nice. You want it. Suddenly it's r decision. I get to be Jeffrey.

JEFFREY: Fuck you.

STEVE: Maybe.

JEFFREY: *Maybe?*

STEVE: You know, I think you should woo me. Maybe dinne Maybe dancing.

JEFFREY: Yes!

STEVE: And then . . .

JEFFREY: Unbelievably hot sex!

STEVE: Not yet.

JEFFREY (*very frustrated*): What do you want?

STEVE: Jewelry.

JEFFREY: Yes!

STEVE: No, wait. What did my horoscope say this morning? "You will meet an incredibly fucked-up guy. Happiness is impossible. Go for it."

JEFFREY: Yes! (*After a beat:*) Yes?

STEVE (*after a moment*): Yes.

JEFFREY: But Steve—first you have to promise me something.

STEVE (*exasperated*): *What?*

JEFFREY: Promise me . . . you won't get sick.

STEVE (*after a beat*): Done.

JEFFREY: And you won't die.

STEVE: Never.

JEFFREY (*staring at* STEVE, *very emotional*): Liar.

(JEFFREY*and* STEVE move toward each other. STEVE *pulls back.*)

STEVE: Jesus. We shouldn't do this. We are really asking for it. Give me one good reason. Give me one reason why we even have a prayer.

JEFFREY: You want one good reason?

STEVE: I do.

JEFFREY (*after a beat*): I dare you.

*They stare at each other.* JEFFREY *tosses the balloon to* STEVE. *The balloon almost hits the ground, but* STEVE *leans forward and catches it. He holds the balloon for a moment and then tosses it back to* JEFFREY. *They move upstage and toward each other, tapping the balloon back and forth. The balloon is caught in the light of the moon and glows translucently. Finally,* JEFFREY *catches the balloon. He and* STEVE *embrace and kiss as the lights dim.*

CURTAIN

**PLUME**

# GREAT SHORT FICTION

☐ **MEN ON MEN:** *Best New Gay Fiction* **edited and with an introduction by George Stambolian.** "Some of the best gay fiction, past, present and future . . . It's a treat to have it conveniently collected. And it's a treat to read. Hopefully the word will now spread about the riches of gay writing."—Martin Bauml Duberman                    (258820—$12.00)

☐ **MEN ON MEN 2:** *Best New Gay Fiction* **edited and with an introduction by George Stambolian.** "This collection includes some of the hotest (in other words, coolest) stories I've read anywhere. *Men On Men 2* is a rich late-eighties mix of love and death."—Brad Gooch, author of *Scary Kisses.*
                                                        (264022—$12.00)

☐ **MEN ON MEN 3:** *Best New Gay Fiction* **edited and with an introduction by George Stambolian.** This diverse, collection continues to explore the universal themes of fiction—love, family, and conflict—from the perspectives of such leading authors as Paul Monette, Philip Gambone, Robert Haule, Christopher Bram, and sixteen others.     (265142—$11.00)

Prices slightly higher in Canada.

---

# By the year 2000, 2 out of 3 Americans could be illiterate.

It's true.

Today, 75 million adults . . . about one American in three, can't read adequately. And by the year 2000, U.S. News & World Report evisions an America with a literacy rate of only 30%.

Before that America comes to be, you can stop it . . . by joining the fight against illiteracy today.

Call the Coalition for Literacy at toll-free **1-800-228-8813** and volunteer.

## Volunteer Against Illiteracy. The only degree you need is a degree of caring.